A Thousand Cuts

Andrea Drew

A THOUSAND CUTS

First edition. April 1, 2019.

Written by Andrea Drew.

CHAPTER ONE

SOCIALISING DIDN'T exactly rate at the top of my list, but then as an Australian homicide detective, I didn't get a whole bunch of time at home with my wife and kids, let alone spinning shit with a bunch of strangers.

The last time I'd come close had been at Melbourne Crime Command six months earlier; a few of us had stayed back for drinks. One of the newer detectives told me the murder scenes didn't get to him, he'd acquired the art of detachment. At that point, I knew he was full of shit.

I might have believed him once, might have felt like he did. For almost two decades, I'd kept jobs at arm's length, staying professional, maintaining a sense of distance at the murder scene and during the investigation.

Until the murder of seven-year-old Jessica Holmes.

Some cases stand out. They stay with you. They take a piece of your soul and you never get it back.

Most cops know that detectives give everything they have to each job. We've seen every crime scene, every gruesome discovery, every sick, twisted murder, and witnessed the depths of human depravity countless times.

Then we get the call to another job and our lives are plunged into hell once again.

I'd been a detective sergeant at Crime Command in the central business district of Melbourne for many years. I'd risen through the ranks quickly, and that morning since eight a.m., I'd been working on another job when my desk phone chirped.

"DS Jack Fletcher speaking."

"Jack, got a job for you." I recognised the gravelly voice of Harry Filsche at Knox Crime Investigation Division or CID straight away. Harry was getting close to retirement, early sixties, balding with a hard-won paunch, and a reputation as a good bloke.

Usually homicide crime scenes were attended by cops at the local crime investigation department or CID. From there the jobs are referred to Melbourne crime command in the city.

I rested an elbow on the desk. "Hey, Harry. Where and what?"

"Sherbrooke National Park. Hikers found a body. Called it in. The divisional van's been out, and I've just come back from the scene. Definitely suspicious." Harry paused. "This one's a kid."

An ache formed at the back of my throat. Four days earlier, I'd visited the distraught Holmes family after their daughter Jessica hadn't come home from the park across the road. Her older sister had come home alone. Despite coordinated exhaustive searches by the Police Emergency Service and other volunteers, Jessica hadn't been found. I offered up a silent hope this wasn't her body.

"The team there? Forensics?" I said.

"Yeah, your boss is en route, and the rest of the team. Forensics are setting up. Prepare yourself though. The body's been staged, and the girl was sexually assaulted and tortured before death. She definitely didn't do it to herself." He paused for a moment. "I'll send the GPS location through."

"Okay, I'm on it." I hung up, grabbed my jacket from the back of the chair, scooped up my keys and wallet from the top drawer, and headed for the exit.

"Out on a job, Jerry," I called out to Jerry Wallace, another detective at the desk diagonally across from me. He looked deep in the middle of writing a report.

"Right, Jack." Wallace kept his focus on the keyboard.

I strode down the corridor towards the car park and flicked a glance through the window to the supervisor's desk belonging to Selena Hicks. The desk was empty—as expected.

A slight breeze blew as I pushed the back door open, and my boots crunched on concrete steps as I made my way down. Leaves from the trees and bushes had made their way into the underground car park, as Autumn set in. I'd parked my white Ford Falcon just a few feet away and pushed the remote to unlock it. As I started up the Falcon, my phone pinged. Harry had come through with the GPS location, and I paused to activate the maps function.

Sherbrooke National Park, a huge stretch of government land, covered thousands of acres. The scumbag must have dumped her in there. Murders left an imprint on the soul, but a child—an innocent child—was a category all by itself.

No one liked child killers, not even other crims.

I knew I'd be spending some time in the car, driving from the city to Sherbrooke, so I turned the music up; it was an attempt at distraction but barely made a dent in my mood.

The car stopped at the traffic lights. I knew the route; friends lived in the area and I'd driven through it many times, down the freeway, exiting at Burwood Highway. Then on to the fork in the road at the foot of the mountain, taking a right onto Mount Dandenong Road. I thought about the Holmes family, when I'd visited them last to take Jessica's missing persons report, and I wondered if this body was their daughter.

The Father, Will, had collapsed with grief and fallen from the kitchen chair. I'd used one arm to prop him up so he didn't hit the floor. Once I'd got him seated again, his wife Melinda had arrived a few minutes later; to my shock, she stood and verbally picked Will apart at every opportunity, taking out all her fury on him. And he simply sat there and took it, looking dazed and useless.

Later, when I was alone with Will, I hadn't been surprised when he quietly mentioned they'd separated. Jessica's distressed ten-year-old sister Gemma didn't fare so well either. She said when she'd stopped playing, she couldn't find her sister. And as most cops know, when missing children don't turn up later that night, the best time to find them alive is in the hours that follow, not four days later.

I attempted to shift my attention from the new job in Sherbrooke to other things, but all I could think of was Will Holmes, and how he'd react if the body did turn out to be his beloved daughter.

Light traffic meant I reached the location in reasonable time. I turned into the parking area, usually empty and currently filled with the forensic team's vehicles, a marked police car, and Ed Garrett's unmarked Falcon.

I trekked across from the car park down a slight slope and towards a clearing, a path worn down by thousands of footsteps and leading in about a kilometer, until I saw the tape. A uniformed officer stood guard at the scene.

It was Constable Gary Webb. Normally, we'd have smiled at each other. Today, I knew no smiles would be on anyone's face. I flashed my badge according to protocol. Webb wrote down my details on his clipboard and waved me through. My knees brushed against bushes laced with dew hanging across the dirt path.

In front of me now stood Andy Collen, another crime command detective sergeant, just a hundred metres or so ahead. He rubbed his face. His suit looked rumpled and a two-day growth darkened his cheeks and chin. Collen nodded as he caught sight of me.

"Worked through again, eh?" I said, slightly out of breath as I reached his side.

Collen grunted. Judging by the redness of his face and the pressure building behind it, he struggled to keep himself together. Considering he'd been a homicide detective for as long as me—nearly twenty years—that was saying something. I gazed about to take in the surroundings, looking for either Gary Holmberg—one of our homicide detectives—or Selena Hicks, Team Leader and the immediate superior to many of us.

I spotted Selena head down in conversation with a forensic technician about thirty metres away. Another officer, Detective Sergeant Ed Garrett, stood over by the body.

"What we got, Ed?" I called as we drew closer, wondering if he'd even manage a response.

"Little girl tortured then murdered," Garrett looked at the ground. I began lifting my knees high to get through the growth and head towards the body, and grass swished behind me as Collen followed.

"Rough one, huh?" We'd reached the body now, and there was silence in the forest other than the occasional call of a lone lyrebird.

"I've got kids, like you," Collen said. "A little girl. Could be my daughter. It's not easy when it's a kid."

"Yeah." I rubbed a light sheen of sweat from my forehead. The body lay in a clearing, naked, with blonde hair splayed on the forest floor. A knot formed in my stomach. I couldn't help noticing she had the same colour hair as my youngest daughter, Maddy, except lighter blonde streaks were running through the dead girl's hair.

My throat ached, and I swallowed hard. This little girl had been tortured before death, her body littered with what looked like small cuts and cigarette burns. Naked, her hands had been folded across her chest, possibly deliberately staged. We both stared at the body for what seemed to be a long time but was probably no more than thirty seconds.

I'd been proud that, as a homicide detective of nearly two decades, I'd become acclimatised to most crimes, more professional, more focused. And all those illusions were now shattered.

The cuts on the girl's body covered almost every available inch of skin. Cigarette burns littered her torso. This little girl hadn't just been murdered, she'd suffered a slow agony of torture.

"Sexual assault?" I called to Ed. It took a while before he responded.

"Possibly, the government pathologist's about to transport the body. I know there's sickos out there, but this... I've never seen anything like this..." Ed's voice didn't increase in volume.

"Yeah." I did my best to quell the queasiness rising in my gut. "Not looking forward to telling the Holmes family."

"You know this girl?" said Ed, taking a step closer in my direction.

"Jessica Holmes. Parents reported her missing four days ago."

Both of us knew how that would go, having done countless notifications. I'd been in daily contact with Jessica's parents, and police emergency services combined with local volunteers had searched every inch of the park where she'd disappeared, as well as the surrounding areas. As a parent myself, I'd made it a point to visit Jessica's father daily and his face had become a deeper shade of ash with each passing day.

Will had asked me to make a promise I'd find her. I knew better than to make one I couldn't keep but I did promise to do everything in my power to find his daughter.

I hadn't wanted to say out loud what we both already suspected; if Jessica hadn't been found on the first day, we most likely wouldn't find her alive.

"Shit," Collen said, staring at a point in the distance. "The media's here."

A truck rumbled into the car park, most likely Ted Richards from Channel Six. Ted had a reputation for pushing his luck with investigations, and I'd snuck him snippets of information in the past when it suited me, but this was pushing our agreement too far. No way in hell would he get information before the body had been identified, or the family contacted.

I breathed deeply through my nose, attempting to quell the rising nausea.

"I'll sort this out," I strode back towards the car park, arms swinging. I heard Ed's footsteps behind me.

"Leave it, mate, let the boss sort it out. Better we talk to the techs, then the government pathologist. Don't get into it." I ignored him, increasing my pace.

I was primed and ready for Ted Richards. I pushed up the police tape and strode towards the car park. Richards, tall, thin and grey-haired, stood with his microphone primed next to the blue and white truck with its satellite dish perched on top.

Unbelievable.

The gravel of the car park crunched under my feet as I increased my strides. Richards lowered the microphone for a moment.

"Jack, any comment on the case?" he said, gripping his microphone. I stopped inches away, glaring at him, shoving balled fists into my pockets. Maybe that way, I'd be less inclined to break his nose. Richards and I had shared an uneasy alliance over the years. I'd given him one or two exclusives when it suited my purposes, so it seemed he now thought it gave him carte blanche to call me in repeated attempts at getting inside information. I more often than not knocked him back. Over the years, we'd fallen into what I'd foolishly assumed was some kind of understanding.

"You couldn't have called?" A muscle flickered in my left cheek.

Richards smiled, but it looked more like a grimace. "You wouldn't answer my call, Jack, let's be honest. All bets are off on this one, a child has been killed and we both know what that means." I unclenched and reclenched my fists, pushing them further down into my pockets.

"How did you know it involved a child, Ted?"

"I never disclose my sources." I wanted to wipe the smug look off Richards' face and swallowed the burning rage rising up through my chest. Collen stood at my side, and muttered quietly, "Easy, Jack, he's not worth it."

Birds chirped, breaking the silence in what would otherwise have been a peaceful location.

Surrounded by sublime rainforest, I still wanted to punch the man's lights out.

"Our media unit deals with this type of thing," I said, taking a large breath of rainforest air. "You really think we're going to give you information on an active case before the government pathologist's been and the victim has been identified? Before the family's been notified? Seriously?"

Richards reddened. I took a step closer, almost nose to nose with him. Collen placed his hand on my right arm.

Footsteps crunched on the gravel behind us, and Selena Hicks stopped to my left, not making eye contact; rather, she fixed her gaze on Ted Richards, and his cameraman, Jethroe.

Selena Hicks—or boss lady—had a reputation as a formidable force now she was Team Leader, and definitely not someone to be tangled with.

She'd risen through the ranks from a rookie, to the Drug Squad, to Homicide and eventually as Team Leader within the department in record time. She and I had worked together for a few years now, and although she gave me a fairly relaxed leash, I didn't want to overstep the mark too much. The slack leash was the only thing preventing me from punching Richards' lights out.

She was shorter than me but—judging by her hands-on-hips stance—seemed to have no sense of being any smaller than her subordinates. She led with her chin, or in her case, her hawk-like nose. I'd figured early on that it might have been the reason she'd been dubbed 'The Hawk.'

Selena Hicks, meanwhile, stood by watching it all. She observed the situation with intense ferocity.

"Mr. Richards," she said, her lips thinned and baring her teeth in what might have appeared to Richards to be a smile. I knew it as a warning sign to run as far away as humanly possible. "All media enquiries are handled by our media unit, as I'm sure you're aware."

The placatory smile had vanished from Richards' own face. He appeared unsure, palms up.

"No offence intended; just doing our job," he said. The cameraman lowered the camera from his shoulder, and it hovered over the case a step behind him.

"So, you'll understand we need to do ours. No details are provided on an ongoing investigation, particularly in such early stages. Our media unit will be in touch," said Selena between gritted teeth.

Jethroe looked in Richards' direction for a clue as to what to do next, eyes wide. "We'll just wait here then, if you could notify your media unit?" He appeared to have rallied from his initial surprise at the appearance of the big boss from Homicide.

"Mr. Richards," Selena said. "The government pathologist will be removing the body in due course. As you can see, there is limited space in the car park, as it's a small area usually frequented by hikers. I'd appreciate it if you could move on to allow space for forensics to do their job." She glared at him, and Richards' adam's apple bobbed up and down.

"Last I checked, this area was public property," he said. I shut my eyes and grimaced, before opening them up with a grin. Ted Richards had decided to push his luck. What a surprise.

"Are you blind, Mr. Richards?" Selena gestured towards the car park, where vehicles were packed tightly, just millimetres between them. "This is a crime scene. The government pathologist's vehicle will need to leave, and with your truck here, access is not exactly unimpeded. I'll tell you again; pack up and vacate this crime scene now, or I'll consider charges of obstructing an investigation."

"Is that a threat?" he muttered, but his face had reddened, and with a raise of his chin, he indicated that Jethroe should pack up the camera. Jethroe lifted the handle of the camera case and walked back to the Channel Six truck.

"That's not a threat, it's a promise." Hicks's hands had moved from her hips to gesticulating wildly.

Ted muttered something unintelligible, and finally conceding defeat, turned and walked slowly back to the van. Then Hicks turned in my direction.

"Head back to Crime Command, Fletcher, you're no good here," she said, her eyes boring holes into my face.

"The crime scene's just been set up, and it's a kid, a girl..." I swallowed hard to push down the gristle that had formed in my throat.

"I know. We're all struggling, but head back, Jack, not here, not now." The lines on her face relaxed.

"Just a few more minutes, then I'll get out of here." I rubbed the back of my neck with my right hand.

"No Jack, now." She stared at me, giving me the frown reserved for special occasions. There was no sense in arguing the point.

Collen nodded and lifted his hand briefly in a goodbye, then headed back to the crime scene.

I stormed back to the car, ignoring the Channel Six cronies. Jethroe offered a pathetic attempt at a wave from the passenger-side window of the truck as it rumbled past.

As I reached the car, I pointed the remote control button at it, unlocked it and swung in. I sat for a moment, clenching my teeth before swearing. I let what I'd just witnessed sink in, but pictures of the scene pushed their way in, the tortured body of Jessica Holmes.

The fact the fragile body had been left naked wasn't what stayed with me, it was the countless tiny cuts all over her tiny and lifeless frame. None of them looked like they'd taken her life, but if she'd been alive at the time, each cut would have inflicted unimaginable pain upon an innocent child.

I focused on my breathing in an attempt to slow it down and restore calm, a return to normality. But nothing would ever be normal about this case, nothing.

I screamed, not caring who heard me, a rage of red flashing before my eyes. I punched the steering wheel over and over. The frustration—the ache of a child's tortured body, and knowing that once her identity was confirmed, I'd need to notify the Holmes family—welled up inside my chest until it came thrashing out.

After I'd vented my fury and finished screaming and pounding the steering wheel, my breathing came in ragged gasps, and I leaned back against the driver's seat, looking at the car roof. As I turned the key in the ignition. I wondered if concentrating on getting through traffic would bring me closer to the present, rather than speculating on the worm that would torture, rape and kill a child.

To a degree, it worked, although not completely. The monotony of driving and trying to stay in the present helped turn the picture of Jessica's body from full colour to monochrome, but it didn't eradicate the dread of notifying Will Holmes that his daughter had been tortured, raped and murdered.

As I reached the central business district, I imagined how I'd feel if anything happened to Maddy or Molly, my young daughters, and my chest seemed to give way and disintegrate.

I turned up the radio, hoping the inane chatter from radio hosts would lift my mood. Yet another fail.

I reached Crime Command and pulled into the underground car park, slamming the car door shut and ran towards the basement lift. As the lift lurched, my stomach lurched too, and queasiness took hold.

I punched the numbers on the keypad so hard that I wondered if they'd fall off, I noticed the office was almost empty; most of the staff had been called out. As I lunged over to my desk, the queasiness became fully-fledged nausea, and my stomach spasmed. I threw my right hand over my stomach, using my left to steady myself on my office chair.

Shit.

I ran to the bathroom, kicked open a stall door and threw up, like a rookie cop at his first crime scene.

CHAPTER TWO

ALTHOUGH STRICTLY SPEAKING, Hicks had sent me back to the office to calm down, I figured a visit to the Coroner's office nearby wouldn't break too many rules.

After throwing up, I sucked in some much-needed breaths, splashed cold water on my face, and headed back to my desk. I figured that—due to Missing Persons and Homicide sharing the same offices—I'd soon be notified once the body of Jessica Holmes had arrived at the Coroner's office.

Most likely, it was there by now. So, I decided on another course of action.

AFTER FLASHING MY BADGE at the lobby in the government pathologist's building and Coroner's office, and signing in, I took the lift to level five.

I pushed open a glass door and stood in the small reception area, at that time completely unmanned. I pressed the buzzer and looked around while waiting for one of the technicians to grant me access. The place wasn't much bigger than a dog box, with room for two basic chairs, a small table, a plant with leaves browning at the edges and the receptionist's desk.

The government pathologist's office was chronically overworked and undermanned; so I figured an in-person visit would possibly get me faster answers. The staff working there were good people; they'd trained for years to help identify the dead on a salary that didn't exactly run to the high life. An older man, possibly early fifties, with short-cropped grey hair opened the frosted glass door slightly.

"Can I help you?," he said. I hadn't dealt with this guy before, so didn't know him by name. I dragged the badge out of my inside jacket pocket and flipped the case open.

"Detective Sergeant Jack Fletcher," I said. "I'm hoping to gain some information about the child's body—the young girl that arrived this morning—before I notify the family."

"Oh," he said, his expression unreadable. "That one, yes. I'm Ian Foster. Come in, and I'll give you the information I have at hand, although we're still at the preliminary stages."

"Thank you," I said, rubbing the photograph of Jessica Holmes that I'd taken from the file and nestled into the right pocket of my trousers. Somehow, it seemed important to keep her picture with me at all times.

Foster went ahead, and I followed. We treaded quietly down a corridor and entered a room through the third door on the right. Little effort had been made to mask the smell of decomposition, a combination of putrefied garbage and sweet, rotting sewage. Although government pathologists were most likely accustomed to it to some degree, I wasn't, so I noticed it immediately. I'd smelled a fair few dead bodies in my career, but the accumulated stench of a mortuary was something else.

"In here," Foster said as we took another right off the first room.

This one was spacious, but just like all the other government pathologists' exam rooms I'd ever been in; it was plain and sterile, filled with sinks, light blue tiles and trolleys full of what looked like medical equipment. A large hoist hung from the ceiling.

Thankfully, the body of the girl had been covered with a sheet, so the countless torturous cuts were no longer visible. I stood by her face and pulled the photograph from my pocket, showing it to Foster.

"This is Jessica Holmes; her parents reported her missing four days ago."

He paused. "That certainly looks like her. I'll need to confirm identification with the parents—if you can arrange that, please."

"I'll talk to the parents," I said quietly. "Do you have a cause of death yet?" The question barely needed to be asked, judging by the noticeable ligature marks I'd seen earlier across her neck and wrists.

"Asphyxiation," he said. "Time of death most likely sometime late yesterday, but I'll have a more precise date and time of death once the autopsy's complete."

"The cuts and the cigarette burns, were they inflicted while she was alive or post mortem?"

Foster gave me a piercing look as he focused on the other side of the table. "At first inspection, it appears so...I mean, when she was alive. I'll know more once we've done the autopsy."

The anger, the anguish—and the desire to find the disgusting piece of shit that had done this—grew the more I learned. I tried not to think about the screams, the pain a seven-year-old girl went through as she was tortured.

"Any signs of sexual trauma?" I said, hoping in one way the answer was no, but in another yes; if she had been sexually assaulted, DNA from hairs or semen could help us find the killer.

"Yes, unfortunately, it does appear so. I've taken samples for DNA testing, but as you know, DNA testing takes time."

I didn't want to push the process too much. I'd asked for rush testing on DNA before, but it didn't always happen due to backlogs. "Do what you can, Ian, it will help us find a child killer, and a paedophile."

"Like I said, it takes time. I can make a note on the paperwork though," he said, retrieving an instrument from the trolley and pausing over the body. He must have somehow picked up that this case had affected me differently, despite many years investigating homicides.

"No clothes though, nothing left at the scene. What do you make of that?" I said.

Foster had put down the scalpel, most likely intuition telling him it might be better to do it after I left. "It's still early days."

Something *pinged*, an internal alarm that wouldn't shut down. Although still early days, intuition and experience told me this wasn't the murderer's first kill. I couldn't pin it down and had no evidence whatsoever but felt certain this bastard had done this before and would do it again.

Foster was a pathologist, so to a certain extent I'd have been better off running these ideas past Collen or Holmberg, but—for now—Foster was there, and he would have some knowledge of murder, even if from a different perspective. "Seen anything like this before?"

Bent over Jessica's blonde head, Foster paused, his fingertips combing her hair, looking for debris. He turned to face me. "Like what? Torture? The fact that she's a child?"

I had no idea if he played dumb or had had enough of humouring me and wanted to get back to work.

"Doesn't it strike you as odd? Something not right?" I mumbled, rubbing at my chin. "Fairly heinous crime, torture of a young innocent child. Experience tells me these killers work up to this type of thing, start off less intense, then need to make their victim suffer and drag out the murder. It escalates. The ligature marks on her wrists and neck almost look like she was crucified, hung on a cross or something like it."

"Maybe," said Foster. "Fortunately, I don't see too many children in my line of work, but yes, the ligature marks are consistent with that method of death, certainly."

I moved my hands to my hips, took a deep breath and focused my thoughts. "So, this piece of shit rigs up a makeshift cross, and hangs her from it. Wouldn't be a quick death, or I wouldn't have thought so; how long d'you reckon, Doc?"

"I wouldn't like to speculate," said Foster, his voice dropping in pitch and volume, although the sound still echoed through the tiled and cavernous room.

"I figure this wasn't a one-off. The perpetrator worked up to this. Maybe the first time he killed them too quickly, and now he wanted to take his time, make her suffer."

Foster paused for a moment, frowning. "I've seen a couple of children's cases like that in the last few months, both young girls, roughly the same age as this one."

"Oh yeah?" I took a step forward, removing my hands from my hips and shifting them to my pockets. "What kind of cases?" Sounded like there'd be a task force forming up fairly soon if that were the case. I'd check with Jerry Wallace at Crime Command.

He shook his head. "I don't remember exactly, too many cases to keep track of, but I do remember the children. In the last few weeks, I've seen two of them, girls around the same age."

"Same injuries?" I said quietly.

"No, the other girls were stabbed. I'm sorry I can't remember the name of the officer in charge, but I think it was a woman."

"Thanks I'll look them up." I said.

"Of course," said Foster.

"Ever wondered if these murders are from the same killer? The first two murders, the girls were stabbed, which would have been a faster kill; maybe he wanted to slow it down a bit?" I said.

"I don't know," he said. "They seem completely different."

"Sexual trauma?"

"I think so, but I'd need to look them up." He moved back to examine the marks around Jessica Holmes' left wrist.

The truth was, no matter how long I hung around the government pathologist's office, I couldn't delay the inevitable for much longer. I had to visit the family, let them know we'd found their daughter's body before the media began pursuing them, and arrange identification of Jessica's body.

"Thank for your help, I appreciate it. I'll see myself out," I said, raising one hand to Foster. As I traipsed from the room and headed back down the corridor, through the door and towards the lift, I wondered who we had that not only had a background of sexually abusing minors, but of murder.

The belief that a serial killer had done this, grew from a kernel at first, then took root. I trudged back towards the car park for the drive back to the office. Most likely, Holmberg or Collen would come with me to notify the parents, but even still, it would be a tough one. Most officers dreaded notifying family of a murder.

Jessica had been playing at the park in Croydon, across the road from her home, with her sister Gemma, and both children were in the care of their father. As a result, Melinda Holmes didn't exactly hold back in naming the one she blamed for her daughter's disappearance.

Now the body had been found, not only would I need to notify the family, but I knew we'd need to eliminate the parents as suspects early on, as we always did in murder cases.

I drove back to Crime Command, wondering if Collen and Holmberg were in the office so I could coordinate the notification visit.

CHAPTER THREE

I KNEW I COULD COUNT on Ed Garrett. As soon as I'd asked him to come along to the Holmes' family home for the notification, he'd agreed in a heartbeat. Holmberg had been called out onto a case, so Garrett and I had also asked a junior detective, Steve Lamont, to come with us, even if he did shift his gaze and wring his hands at the prospect. It paid to have a few officers there, particularly in a sensitive case like this one, where the wife could possibly turn on the estranged husband. It was also good to have help on hand to call other family members if more support was needed.

The Holmes family address was located in Croydon, a twenty minute drive from the crime scene, and a longer drive from Crime Command in the city.

After parking our vehicles out the front, I locked the car. Lamont and Garrett out of their vehicle and followed. I pushed open the white gate, which creaked as I nudged it with my knee. The lawn was overgrown, although flowers peeked out from various well-pruned bushes. The front curtains twitched and a couple of seconds later, a lock turned and the handle on the screen door jiggled slightly.

Leaves covered the wooden porch. I stood in front of the screen door, Garrett, and Lamont standing either side, having climbed the two steps to flank me. Will Holmes opened the screen door for us to enter. His eyes were wide, and he looked like he'd had a rough night, unshaven and with red-rimmed eyes, t-shirt creased, chestnut hair rumpled, and dark crevasses for eye sockets.

I wondered if he'd worked out for himself what we were about to tell him, considering three cops had turned up? I'd sent him a text the night before, to let him know I'd be paying him a visit the following morning.

Judging by the fact Jessica hadn't been found, he'd probably had a fairly good idea of the content of our upcoming conversation.

"Come in," he mumbled before disappearing back inside to the semi-darkness. I looked at Garrett and Lamont, stepping inside as my eyes adjusted to the darkened room with its closed curtains.

Since the last time I'd visited, Will Holmes had tried to clean the place, and the takeaway containers were no longer covering every surface but the smell in the place remained, a combination of unwashed clothes and general stuffiness.

Will sat down at the freshly-wiped pine kitchen table, and I took a seat across from him. Garrett and Lamont loitered around the living area, hands in pockets, glancing uneasily at the front door.

Will looked at me. "Melissa's on her way." His low, quiet voice and the slight waver in its tone told me he'd guessed correctly on the subject matter of our conversation.

I took a deep breath. "I'm not sure how to tell you this, and we will need you to identify her but...we think we found Jessica's body in Sherbrooke National Park. I'm so sorry."

Will Holmes' eyes closed, his head went down and he fell forward in the chair, knees lowering. He almost connected with the floor, sliding away. I caught him under one arm, lifted him up and helped him sit back up. Now, he began sobbing a deep guttural sound. I moved one hand to his shoulder and sat quietly as the sobs racked his body. It took some time before he was able to speak.

"My girl, my Jessie, oh my God," he whispered. "My little girl. Did she suffer?"

"She was raped and killed. I'm so sorry," I decided not to mention the torture.

Will's sobs intensified, and he moaned again, plaintive cries. "My girl, my baby girl. No! What did they do to you, what did they do? I should have been there."

I put my hand on his back. "Please don't blame yourself. No parent imagines anything like this will ever happen to their child."

Lamont moved closer and sat down on the chair opposite me. Garrett moved to the net curtains. I saw a curt nod out of the corner of my eye.

The media had set up camp.

Will Holmes had barely noticed my flicker of distraction. He raised his face, red and drowning in tears. The torture would only come up once the family viewed the body, which was a later discussion to be had. "I'm sorry, I know this is a difficult time, but we'll need to arrange for you to identify here body. Also, if you could answer some questions it will help with the investigation." Lamont had his notepad at the ready.

"Now?," Will said, his lips quivering.

"If we could, while it's fresh in your mind," I said. "It really will help." Ed Garrett had moved closer. "I'll arrange the identification once the media has left." he said.

Will Holmes nodded.

"Okay," he said and stood up, swaying a little as he held onto the table.

I looked around for something to help calm Will down. "Can I pour you a drink?" I said.

"In the cabinet, by the wall," he answered as he moved towards the couch and fell down onto it.

"I'll get it." Garrett had almost reached the cabinet. He found the bottle of whiskey, poured some into a glass and brought it over to Will. He took a sip, and continued staring at the floor, eyes unseeing.

I dragged a pen and small notebook from my jacket pocket. Lamont was also taking notes wide-eyed and seemingly glad of something to do. "I know you told me this once before," I said, "But can you confirm what Jessica was wearing?"

"Jeans, white t-shirt with a Pokémon on it," said Will, his voice cracking.

"And... underwear?" I said, not looking up from my notebook.

"Underwear? Huh?" said Will.

His eyes were red, and he ran fingers through his hair.

"Sometimes, a killer will remove items from the scene, as trophies," I said. Will stared at the floor again.

"Probably the Ben 10 underwear; she was obsessed with it," he said. "She was always a bit of a tomboy," he collapsed into sobs again.

"Can we go over again what happened the day Jessica went missing and what your movements were?" I said.

"Gemma, her sister, was with her that day in the park. It was just across the road I thought it would be okay. I was just coming home from work," Will said quietly.

At that moment, the front door opened and Melinda Holmes entered, with a man behind her. Her blonde frizzy hair looked newly styled, somewhat incongruous under the circumstances. "I bought these for the girls" she said and dropped her bags on the floor. The man, obviously several years younger, stood behind Melinda, shifting his weight from one foot to the other. "What's going on?" she said, looking around at the police in her lounge room, and, her voice rose in pitch.

I stepped forward and extended a hand. She shook it limply and stared about the room. "Mrs. Holmes, you'll remember me, I trust? I'm Detective Sergeant Fletcher, this is DS Ed Garrett, and DC Steve Lamont." They rose and walked towards her but she didn't bother shaking their hands. Her mouth had dropped, eyes wide.

Will gazed over at her, wiping his eyes.

"Will, what the hell is going on?" she said, her voice screeching, rapidly increasing in volume and intensity. "Did you find Jessica? Where is she?"

Will extended a hand out to her. "Melinda, they found her. She's dead. They just arrived to tell me, they want us to identify the body" he said.

The woman began wailing and screaming, her moans bone-shattering. "No!" she screamed. "No, not my girl, bring her back! Bring her back to me!" The young man moved to step beside her, supporting her as she fell to her knees and began rocking back and forth.

Garrett and Lamont moved closer to her, and Melinda Holmes began lashing out and screaming. "No, it's not true, I don't believe you. If something had happened to her, I would know!"

She was inconsolable. I spoke quietly into Will Holmes' ear "Does she have a doctor? Someone we can call to prescribe her something?"

"Yeah, Dr Baker in Knox," he said. "I'll call him now."

The younger man began speaking to Melinda, attempting to calm her down. I still had no idea who the man was, so I moved closer. Garrett and Lamont held Melinda gently to stop her from hurting herself. After a while, she calmed a little, and allowed the younger man—presumably her new boyfriend—to guide her towards the stairs.

"Can I talk to Gemma?" I said to Will, who'd just finished his telephone call.

"She's at her Nanna's, back tomorrow" he mumbled.

I was momentarily distracted, feeling the need to ID the man before he disappeared with Melinda. "Excuse me," I called out. I noticed he stopped and looked back in my direction. "Could I talk to you briefly?"

"Now?" The man paused, one foot on the stair above. He turned and peered through the railings on the staircase.

"I won't keep you for long, just standard procedure." He sighed as if I had asked something unacceptably irritating as he stepped back down into the living area.

He didn't sit at the table with Will and me, instead hovering nearby with his hands shoved into his jeans.

"The first obvious question is," I began, "Who are you?"

His eyebrows raised and he looked away, not caring to respond. I waited it out. There was a definite need to know who was wandering about.

"Eric," he said.

"Eric? Eric what? And what is your relation to the family?"

"Eric Slavosky. Not any relation. I'm Melinda's partner." He stared me in the eye as if willing me to look away or challenge him.

"Any ID on you, Eric?" I asked, adding a slight smile to try and soften the situation. He took a small leather wallet from his back pants pocket and opened it, the same way I'd flash my own ID badge. There, in the front plastic sleeve of the wallet, was his driver's license. I took a close look and handed the wallet back.

"Fine," I said. "Thanks. Now that's out of the way, Eric, can you remember your movements four days ago, on 12th March?"

"What, you think I had something to do with this?" Eric raised his eyebrows again and leaned forward at the waist, his neck jutting out.

"Eric, it's just standard procedure to eliminate those in the victim's close social circle. I'd just like to eliminate you from our enquiries early on. I'll be asking everybody else exactly the same. So, 12th March, where were you?"

"What day was that?"

"Last Thursday morning."

Eric frowned. "Ah yes, Thursday I remember. Melinda was discharged from hospital, and I was there. Waited around for a couple of hours while they completed the paperwork."

"Thank you," I wrote it in my notebook. "Name of the hospital?"

"Pinewood Private." Eric cleared his throat. "Now if you'll excuse me, Melinda needs me."

"Of course," I said, adding the hospital name to my list of enquiries to follow up on. Eric slouched away towards the stairs.

I turned my gaze back to Will Holmes. "Will your ex-wife be okay?"

"Yeah," he said. "Dr Baker's on the way over to calm her down, but then she wasn't exactly stable anyway. For once, Eric the prick's made himself useful."

"We'll need to stay until the media unit arrives." I said.

"All right," said Will.

Obviously, there was no love lost between Will Holmes and Eric, the new boyfriend. Garrett and Lamont stood to my right, murmuring to each other, the conversation barely discernible.

Garrett walked towards me and edged up close to my right side. "Hicks sent me a text, media unit alert. Bit late, but..."

I hung my head. We weren't going anywhere in a hurry. Lamont took a step away diagonally, then turned. "Hamburger with the lot?"

"Yeah, mate." Not that I was hungry, exactly, but we all knew we were in for a late finish. I walked over to the couch and sat down. I withdrew my phone from the inside pocket of my jacket and typed out a text, not easy considering my mutton fingers.

Late home, probably tonight's news, I texted.

Another night at work. I barely knew my daughters' schedules these days, let alone Abbie's. She'd be fine, though. Thankfully, I'd married an independent and capable woman—even if things had been strained between us lately, thanks to the ever-increasing demands on my time and energy.

Garrett had his notepad out, taking notes, most likely orders for the night's dinner. He passed it to Lamont and nodded silently.

I thought about what I needed to do. I planned on going over the crime scene photos one more time, and following up on the whereabouts of Will, Melinda and Eric, as well as speaking to Gemma again.

I handed my card to Will, telling him to call me anytime, night or day. He dropped his head in a semblance of a nod.

"We're not going anywhere just yet though," I said. "The media unit will be here soon, so hold tight."

He sat on the couch, hunched over, fists on his head, and sobbed. I told him I'd see him the next day to talk to Gemma, and he nodded, barely looking up.

Tracey and a colleague from the media unit arrived much later that night. After giving her a brief rundown of the situation in a hushed voice, she nodded.

I signalled to the other detectives that we should leave and opened the front door. We headed back to our parked cars.

"See you back at Crime Command," said Garrett, and I nodded, knowing we couldn't say a great deal within distance of the Holmes family.

I wondered what additional information Gemma had; for some reason, during her initial questioning I'd got the impression she was holding something back. Potentially, her information could change the whole direction of the case. She hadn't been there earlier. Will had possibly had a warning of what was coming and had sent her away for a day or two.

Arriving back at Crime Command, I threw my jacket over the back of the chair and grabbed the information we had so far. The photos were as horrifying as ever. The tiny cuts all over her body, the burn marks, her tiny naked body posed with her hands crossed over her chest... it all hit me like a physical blow.

What kind of monster did this to a child? Whoever it was, they'd worked up to this, until the killing no longer satiated their sick desires.

Starting with the basics, I began a basic timeline of dates, starting with Jessica's visit to the park and through to the day her body was found.

I'd checked with Will Holmes on his whereabouts the day his daughter disappeared, and he had a fairly decent alibi; he'd been at work, something that could easily be checked. Gemma, Jessica's sister, could possibly hold the key, especially if she'd been at the park with her. If Jessica had left with someone, Gemma could possibly identify them. I'd also need to confirm with Pinewood Private that Melinda had been discharged the day we'd found Jessica's body, and—importantly—we had to know that Eric was definitely with her at the time.

I searched on my computer for cases involving the murder of a child, a young girl, in the area. There'd been few murders of children, but a couple of others had appeared over recent months, both of them young girls, although a few years older than Jessica.

I looked them up. Both girls had been stabbed and the bodies moved and staged after death. Both had appeared in various locations within the Sherbrooke forest area, within the Dandenong ranges shire.

The hairs on the back of my neck stood up. My belief that this was the work of a serial killer seemed to be drawing closer to confirmation.

The cases were still open and unsolved. Ten year old Taylor Wentworth was a ward of the state. She'd been found stabbed a couple of months earlier, body staged. Eleven year old Bianca Baker had vanished from a shopping centre, and her body was found two weeks later, stabbed and body staged within a different section of Sherbrooke Forest.

Both murders happened a couple of months earlier. Despite some initial coverage, the media barely mentioned them these days. The initial calls had come through from a Detective Sergeant Rae Swanson of the Ringwood branch, within the Maroondah jurisdiction. I looked her up and called her. It went to voicemail. In the meantime, I'd pull the files for the murders of Taylor and Bianca, and get a board started. For Jessica, it would be back to basics and to a timeline of events before heading back to the Holmes family tomorrow to talk to Gemma.

CHAPTER FOUR

THE SKY WAS AS DARK as ink when I finally called it a night and arrived home, but some of the lights inside were still on.

Despite declining her calls, Abbie must have been waiting up for me. If she wanted an argument at this time of night, I didn't think it would end well; it never did.

The job took its toll on our marriage, but after fifteen years together, I figured maybe she knew what she was up for by now. I assumed she'd been warned beforehand what life as a police wife would be like. Maybe she'd believed she could change me, buoyed along by love and hope. The first few years had been okay. Until I'd transferred to Homicide, that is.

Abbie had the front door open as I reached the porch and walked through. She glared at me, not saying a word. It slammed shut behind me with a heavy thud.

Exhausted, I reached the living room and sat down in one of the chairs, kicking off my shoes with a sigh. They landed with a clatter on the polished floorboards. Through the archway, I saw the fruits of Abbie's eternal organisational skills on the kitchen bench, lunch boxes packed and ready to go into the refrigerator, and school uniforms laundered and ready for the morning.

No question at all she was a damn good mother, and in the moments where I managed some brief flashes of insight, I saw that Abbie was also a pretty patient wife considering she rarely saw me. I should have asked more questions, but then hindsight is a wonderful thing. I was sure she'd talked to police wives before we'd got married, back in the heady days when we socialised at barbeques and gatherings; that was back when life didn't revolve around solving murders day in day out, let alone murders involving hideous brutality against children.

I couldn't be certain I'd get the words out. I lay with my eyes half closed, legs stretched out, and for a moment I paused as the heat from the open fire radiated into my legs. Maybe she wouldn't take it further. Maybe she'd let me be. The brief delusion didn't last long though.

"Did you decline my calls? Again? What the hell is wrong with you?" Lulled into a false sense of security, I'd barely heard her move from the kitchen to the living area. She stood, leaning over me, her face red, hand outstretched, pleading, angry, betrayed—all the usual.

I didn't have much of a defence, other than the brutality of Jessica Holmes's crime scene.

"I'm sorry, I wasn't in a good frame of mind at the time. I thought it was better to decline the call," I said, hoping that would be enough.

"Oh well, I was having a dandy old time, running around doing errands for all of us, you included. I actually called to remind you tonight was Maddy's concert."

I closed my eyes. Shit. I'd missed my girl's big moment. Again.

"Oh God, I'll have to go see her." Unable to move or think too much, I couldn't croak out any more than that.

"She's asleep, Jack. I have a hard enough job explaining why you're working all the damn time. I'm tired of explaining why they can't wait up for you. I'm tired of explaining why you never come to any of their special nights even though you always promise you'll be there. She has school tomorrow and needs to sleep. If you want to see her, you should be home earlier. And I'm tired of saying that too."

Without moving, I managed another couple of words. "I'll go up and kiss her goodnight." In my mind, I tried to work up the energy to get myself up and out of the chair, to go and sit by my beautiful blonde girl and gaze at her for a while, even if she would never know I'd been there.

"I'm practically a single mother, Jack," Abbie sighed, and her anger appeared to have reduced from raging to a quiet simmer. She sat down on the seat opposite, hands on her lap. She looked tired, haggard, her dirty blonde hair floating around her thin face in wisps where it had escaped from the ponytail.

"I got called out to a crime scene today. A little girl, Maddy's age, seven. Raped, tortured beyond all recognition and murdered. That's all." I rubbed my eyes, but that wouldn't erase the scene from my mind. "If someone gave me a choice, and promised to erase the memory from my mind, I'd take it in a heartbeat."

Abbie fell back in the chair. She stayed silent for a long time.

"Oh, God, Jack, I don't know what to say."

There was nothing she could say, and we both knew it. She moved slowly in my direction, staring at me, before sitting beside me on the couch. She reached out tentatively and rested her right hand on my arm. I should probably have shifted my gaze from the floor, where I stared unseeing, but I couldn't look at her.

All I wanted was to see my girls, check on them, hold their hands, warm and full of life, and remind myself that some good still existed in the world. I had two girls that loved me no matter what and who were happy to see, me no matter how many times work called me out to investigate the unthinkable atrocities of which mankind was capable.

"Do you want to talk about it?" she said quietly.

"No, I'm sorry. I don't think I can."

"Okay."

I finally got up from the couch and walked over to the stairs. Abbie stood up and called out to me.

"Jack, please; let's talk. I'm sorry but, you know, I need someone too. We need each other. Talk to me."

But I kept on climbing the soft beige carpet until I reached the upstairs landing. The soft sounds of my daughters' relaxed breathing echoed out from the bedroom doors.

I pushed open the door to Maddy's room. Moonlight streamed in through the gap in the curtains. She looked peaceful, not a care in the world. She lay with one hand out just in front of her face, as if catching a ball in her sleep.

Her blonde hair had the same streaks, as light as sunbeams in places, as the hair of Jessica Holmes. Memories of the crime scene intruded, pushing their way in, and I focussed instead on my daughter's breathing, relaxed and easy, as regular as her heartbeat.

I tried not to think about what Will Holmes would be going through, every parent's worst nightmare. He too would have memories, but memories were no consolation for a little girl that would never come back, never hold him and look at him as the hero she knew him to be—a little girl who would never laugh, play, and run as little girls loved to do.

Something about the abused innocence, the abuse of trust she must have experienced, riled me, rising up through my bones like boiling oil. I couldn't remember ever wanting to catch a perpetrator as badly as I did in this case.

I sat down carefully on the side of Maddy's bed slowly, not wanting to wake her. I traced a line on her palm, skin warm to the touch. As I gazed at her, her skin slowly shifted and morphed into something else, something strange and macabre. A ligature mark began forming on her wrist, a burn mark on her forearm, closely followed by another on her neck, then on her other arm.

I wasn't conscious of my breath, but as I stood up quickly, electricity jolting through me, I realised it came in rasped ragged gasps and my pulse raced. As I took a step back from the bed, I knew it was all just a figment of my imagination.

The ligature marks had disappeared from her wrists, and the burns had miraculously healed over. I leaned over and rested my hands on my thighs, attempting to get a grip on reality and slow my breathing down.

I needed a drink. I walked back down the stairs quietly so as not to wake my daughters and noticed my right hand on the railing shake slightly. I pulled it away, covered the last few steps in record time, and bounded through the lounge room in lengthy strides, relying on a drink to wipe out the memories. Considering I hadn't had one in a long time, it would, I hoped, be an effective amnesiac.

I rifled through the drinks cupboard beside the fireplace, where the fire was now almost burned out.

Abbie sat on one of the armchairs, with the volume to the television down low. "Come to bed, it's late," she said. "I don't want you smelling of drink when I'm trying to sleep." I swallowed an angry retort. What I had to say would only make matters worse.

Instead I found the bottle anyway, wrenched it out of the cupboard, and sat down in the chair closest to the fire. I screwed open the cap of the bottle, lifting it to wipe dust from the label. I took a swig. I'd been expecting that Abbie would try to get me to come to bed but all I wanted was to be left alone with my misery. I'd need to offend her just enough that she should leave me alone yet not so much that she'd never speak to me again.

"I'll get you a glass," she said and disappeared into the kitchen.

She returned and left the glass beside the bottle. I didn't touch it. She sat silently beside me for a while.

"Come to bed Jack, it's late."

"I'm not interested in a night of angry sleeping. Leave me to my bottle and my misery," I said.

That did the trick. Abby spun and headed for the stairs.

It was getting cold now. The scotch tasted better for having sat in the cupboard for months. I took another swig from the bottle. If I was going to sit there for God knew how long, I'd need some heat. I spotted the newspaper and kindling beside the fireplace.

Reluctantly, I pushed myself up and out of the chair leaving the scotch on the hardwood floor momentarily. I scrunched up the newspaper quickly, and shoved balls of it along the bottom before placing kindling on top in no semblance of order. The matches were on the shelf above the fireplace and I lit one and held it in front of a piece of paper until a flame took hold.

Once I was back in the chair, I recommenced my trip down melancholy lane. Today's crime scene wasn't enough to end my career, but it could potentially be marriage-ending. I'd need to do something, some grand gesture, maybe dinner or flowers, something extravagant and unusual. I'd think more about it in the morning; tonight was pretty much a write-off.

Tomorrow, I'd go and visit the Holmes residence, and read the files for the Baker and Wentworth murders if I could get hold of them. The investigation, even in its early stages, hinged heavily on Gemma's memories. Hopefully, she'd seen the man who'd abducted her sister. It was highly unlikely a woman committed the crime; although not impossible, it was rare.

The reassuring and long forgotten sensation of the scotch warming my chest increased in intensity as I took another mouthful.

I turned the lights off and sat back down in the now full darkness of the living room, since Abbie had turned the lights off on her way to bed. Shards of moonlight from the gap in the curtains fell across the floor. Tomorrow, I'd follow up on the other two child murder cases. If I didn't hear back from DS Rae Swanson tomorrow, I'd call her pager; I'd already left her a voicemail and sent a text. I also needed to find out who'd worked the murders here in Crime Command.

I didn't want to think about how Jessica Holmes had felt, what she'd gone through as she'd sustained the countless burn marks on her limbs. How any individual could watch as they inflicted that much pain on a small child was beyond me. As for the ligature marks, they almost looked like she'd been hung up on a cross, one rope on each wrist. I 'saw' Jessica Holmes hanging there, an image I couldn't shake. In my mind, there were two planks of wood to which she was tied, her wrists and ankles bound; her body sagged, putting unknown pressure on her limbs.

Her eyes were red and filled with tears, her energy fading as the last remnants of life prepared to leave. But she was hanging on with all that she had. In my mind, I had found Jessica in time.

"Help me," she said, her voice barely discernible. Instead, the words came out like the mew of a newborn kitten. The cigarette burns were fresh, and spots of blood and pus had begun to form, alongside bruising of every colour. She was in the middle of the forest at Sherbrooke National Park, not a soul in sight.

Who put her there? Where was the killer? No matter; there'd be time for that later. For now, I just had to call an ambulance; if they got here in time, they just might be able to save her.

I looked around for my phone but couldn't see it. Jessica called out to me again, her cries increasingly desperate. The terrain was overgrown, full of long grass, tree ferns, and saplings. Dew hung heavy on the bushes. I propelled myself forward, lifting myself up to a standing position. My feet sank into the mud, but I wouldn't let that stop me. This was my chance, my chance to save her. Despite the mud, I drove myself forward, willing myself to reach her in time and cut her down.

She closed her eyes and dropped her head. This was it. I threw myself at her but landed heavily on the ground. I blacked out at that moment and when I came to, I was back in the lounge room, lying flat across the hardwood floor.

The fire was almost out. It had almost burnt itself down to nothing. I looked in the bottle and saw it was empty. I didn't remember drinking all of it.

So much for drinking to forget. The nightmare had seemed so real but I should've known when I saw Jessica alive, that it was my mind playing tricks. None of it was real. Maybe my desire to erase the memory had caused the vivid nightmare. And somehow, having seen the little girl alive just made my reality worse.

Lying flat on my face in the lounge room, plastered and disoriented, it wasn't my finest moment. I rubbed my face and hoped it wouldn't bruise.

Maybe this was a sign I shouldn't drink, not that I ever paid much attention to signs, only to the harsh reality—and this reality was far too harsh for my liking.

CHAPTER FIVE

WILL HOLMES DIDN'T look any better for the twenty-four hours I'd spent away from him. The dark cavernous bags under his eyes from the day before had now become cavernous suitcases. He didn't look as though he'd slept at all. The three-day growth was now a four-day growth. I couldn't imagine he'd bathed, but then who could blame him considering the circumstances? I shuddered to think how I would react if I lost my Maddy or Molly.

I'd decided to come alone today, figuring I'd get more from him that way. I suspected the day before had overwhelmed him completely, with the number of police officers, the devastating blow of his daughter's death, and his wife's reaction. So, I wanted to keep it more low-key today. It would mean more information, I hoped, and I still believed young Gemma held the key.

After opening the door a crack, Will turned and shuffled back towards the kitchen table. I followed behind him and he pulled out a chair. I sat directly opposite and retrieved the notepad from my jacket pocket.

"How's your ex-wife doing?" I said. I got the impression they hadn't been separated for too long, but I couldn't be sure. Judging by the fact that she had a new boyfriend, possibly enough time had passed that the acrimony might settle down eventually.

"They had to hospitalise her again. Sounds like a nervous breakdown. Doesn't surprise me she didn't take it well, because I was on track to get full custody of the kids, you know. She's had a drinking problem for years," Will said, staring down at the table.

"I'm sorry to hear that," I said.

"So, where is this investigation at?" Will mumbled. "I know it's early days but she's already asking who did it. Even if I can't stand her prick of a boyfriend, it would be nice to give her an answer. She's so paranoid now and jittery about Gemma, she sent him over to stand over and watch Gemma like a hawk. Like—what the hell? Does she think I can't take care of our daughter? If we weren't already separated, we would be by now. She blames me for Jessica's death. Well, just like she blames me for everything else that goes wrong."

I wasn't sure how to respond to that, so figured it was best saying nothing.

"Would it be okay if I spoke to Gemma? At the park they played in? Maybe we could walk there if it's not too far," I said. Besides, I reckoned a short walk might do Will good. Of course, I wouldn't say anything, but it wouldn't surprise me if Will hadn't left the house.

"Yeah, okay. I'll go and send Eric the worm home. They're out in the backyard."

Will got up and traipsed through the doorway behind him, across the kitchen and out to the back patio. He pushed the back door open.

"Gemma!" he called. "Come inside. The detective wants to ask you a few questions, honey."

Gemma ran over, out of breath. She walked across to the table and an anxious look appeared on her face when she saw me.

Gemma's blonde hair fell down her back in waves. Her cheeks were pink, and she was still breathing heavily. She would be their one hope, the one remaining child. My heart melted just seeing her. I could kind of understand why Will's wife Melinda was so possessive of her after the shock of losing Jessica in such horrible circumstances.

Eric followed behind her and headed for the front door. He called out and said goodbye to Gemma and Will, his tone curt, but then there wasn't much love lost between the two men, so it didn't surprise me.

The younger girl stood in front of me and suddenly became shy, her expression changing and eyes downward. She was wringing her hands and shifting her weight from one foot to the other.

"Hi, Gemma," I said. "Thanks for talking to me. This doesn't have to take long but any information you can give me will really help, okay?" I said. Will placed one hand on her right shoulder protectively.

"I'll grab your jacket," said Will. He disappeared and came back with a red duck's down quilted jacket, which he wrapped around her shoulders.

I stood up and shoved the notebook inside my pocket. Then I followed Will and Gemma to the front door.

"It's not far," Will said. "Probably do us good to get out of the house."

We walked about two hundred metres to the park. Will and Gemma didn't speak, so I didn't particularly want to intrude too much. The time for questioning would be once we reached the park.

The park was large with lots of play equipment and a few younger children playing. Gemma walked towards the outskirts of the play area where the fake turf ended, wood chips covering the garden beds.

She seemed nervous, hesitant, like she wanted to play but to do so would be a bad thing. Her father leaned down to whisper in her ear. "It's okay, honey, you're not doing anything wrong; the policeman is here to help," he said. "Tell him everything you can; anything you say will mean he can find the bad man that hurt your sister, okay?"

Gemma continued wringing her hands and looking down at the ground. She didn't seem convinced. "Okay, Daddy," she said quietly. I looked across at Will to reassure him I wouldn't traumatise Gemma.

I squatted down and attempted to get to Gemma's level. Experience had taught me this was the best way to establish rapport.

"Gemma, can you show me exactly what happened on that day? Whether you think it's important or not," I said. I took a deep breath and waited.

"Well, I was... I was playing here. Playing... on the monkey bars. And I noticed Jessica had run off," she said in a quiet voice.

"Okay. What happened next?"

"I was playing with Robbie. When I looked up, Jessica had run to the edge of the park. And she was talking to a man with red hair." She screwed her face up and looked like she was ready to cry.

"You're doing great, Gemma, really great. Do you remember what car he drove? I mean, did you see a car?" I said, trying to keep the intensity of my voice to a minimum. I didn't want to put more pressure on her than she already felt.

"A red truck. I think. I've seen him here before. Other kids got to know him; we called him the puppy man," she said, warming up to the task now.

Now we were getting somewhere.

"What do you mean by the puppy man?" I said. I squatted to look at Gemma's face, squinting as bright sunlight pierced my eyes.

"Everyone knows the puppy man. He comes by the park all the time. He asks if we want to go and see the puppies. Most of us don't go, because…"

She faltered, her eyes beginning to turn red with pent-up tears. Her lip wavered.

"Because what, Gemma?"

She sniffed. Her voice was shaky, and when she spoke again, it was very quiet. I almost couldn't hear her.

"Because…we know not to go with strangers. I should've shouted louder. And I did shout, you know… but she didn't hear me, so I went back to playing. It's all my fault she's dead."

I wanted to comfort her, to reassure her none of this was her fault, but Will had already taken her into his arms and picked her up, holding her close.

"Hey, enough of that," Will said. "None of this is your fault, we all miss her."

Gemma was inconsolable, her wailing increasing in intensity until the sobs that racked her body subsided.

I figured I'd take the opportunity to talk to a few of the children in the playground. I thought about letting Will know of my plans, but he was oblivious, consoling Gemma as best he could.

I walked to the far end of the playground equipment where a diamond-shaped rope climbing frame was the focus. A dark-haired boy stood to one side, watching two other boys attempt to reach the summit.

"Hello," I said. The boy took a small step backwards and eyed me warily.

"It's okay," I said, removing my badge from my coat pocket. "I'm a police officer, see?" The boy peered over and, after staring down his nose at my badge, seemed satisfied. "I'm here about the disappearance of the little girl Jessica, about a week ago. Do you remember it?" I asked.

"Yeah. I remember it," said the boy. "Mum wouldn't let me come down to the park for days. Wasn't really fair, I told her none of us talk to strangers. But Jessica did."

"Can you tell me if you saw the person that spoke to Jessica? Did you see her talk to someone?" I asked, squatting down again.

"Yeah; we all know him. Puppy guy's a creep. I don't know who falls for that line he tries! He's asked me before if I want to come see the puppies. Mum's told me about weirdos like him, and I ran away from him, ran really fast. Jessica should never have talked to him. I mean, it was obvious he was a weirdo."

The kid looked to me to be about twelve but sounded beyond his tender age. A sneaking thought crept into my mind.

"Did you see Gemma call out to Jessica?" I said.

"I saw Gemma playing... but she never called out to Jessica. She just kept on playing," the boy said. I took a step closer.

"Are you sure? It's really important," I said.

"Yeah, I remember because I saw Jessica run over to him, I thought it was weird that Gemma didn't call out to her from the playground, especially when we all know he's a weirdo."

"Thanks," I said. The kid pulled his hands out of his pockets and rubbed them. He scuffed at the bark with one of his boots, before taking hold of his right shoe and removing it to tip bark out.

Turning my head, I saw Will still holding Gemma. He held her face in his hands. I needed to treat this one carefully, but if Gemma was lying about what really happened that day, I needed to know.

"We're heading home," said Will, taking hold of his daughter's hand.

"I have one last question for Gemma, if that's okay," I said, moving closer to where they both stood.

"Gemma, this is important. Did you really call out to Jessica when she ran over to the man? Or did you let her go," I asked quietly.

Gemma kept her head down and wouldn't look at me. I saw Will's grip tighten on her hand, and tension tracked up his arm muscles. I knew he wouldn't like me asking this. But I had to.

"It really is important, Gemma. One of the kids... he said you didn't call out to her, and I'm going to track down some people, but I need to know you're telling the truth," I said.

Will stepped forward a little, in front of his little girl. "Oh, now... you can't..." He sounded horrified, appalled I would put his daughter on the spot. I pretended not to have heard him; Gemma was taking in what I'd said, and in a moment, I knew she would speak. Her breaths were short and panicked, and she whimpered.

Her face crumpled, and she let out a squealing sound. Tears fell down her face.

"This is all my fault. Everyone knows about the puppy man! He's a creep. But I wanted to keep on playing for a while. And I thought she'd be okay, and I never thought something would happen to her...and I didn't call out to her. And I didn't...I didn't... "

She broke down as Will ruffled her hair and held her close. But she hadn't finished. "Gemma?" I said. I touched her lightly on the arm. "You are not in any trouble. You are a brave, brave girl. Just tell me what you did."

She inhaled deeply.

"A couple of minutes later, I turned to where the man had been," she said. "And I looked back at where the creep had been... with his truck... and he was gone! And so was Jessica. So I went home...I *ran* home... to get Dad! Maybe if I'd called out to her, this never would've happened, and she'd still be alive."

Gemma collapsed into a fit of sobs.

Will took hold of his daughter and hugged her again.

"Honey, this is not your fault. Don't think that for a second, Gemma," Will said. He made no effort to keep the anger out of his voice.

"That's more than enough for one day," he told me. "But here's a tip. If you ever do you find the bastard that did this, you better not tell me his name."

I stuffed my hands back in my pockets and stared down at my shoes, before looking back up at Will's tortured face. "Because if I ever find a piece of shit that killed my daughter, I'll kill him myself."

CHAPTER SIX

THE GROTESQUE SIGHT of Jessica Holmes's body hanging on a makeshift cross still wouldn't leave me. I rubbed at my eyes and attempted to run closer, to pull her damn body down and apply CPR, but no matter how hard I tried, I couldn't move.

My shoulder began shaking and my head wobbled. As my eyes slowly opened, I realised I wasn't in Sherbrooke forest. The smell of whiskey didn't belong in a forest. Yet another alcohol-fuelled nightmare. The clock ticked, and I didn't bother looking at the time, the gloom telling me amnesia had taken hold for a few merciful hours. But no matter what, I kept coming back to the same old armchair in the lounge room, with empty bottles littering the living room floor.

I didn't realise Abbie was near until her slippers shuffled behind me. She appeared at the left side of the chair, her hair tousled and her shabby frayed pink dressing gown tied tightly at the waist.

"Jack, what the hell? Did you even sleep at all? Drinking again? This is ridiculous; you need to get help. You're pulling yourself away from life, from living, from your family. Now stop! This has to stop!" Her voice rose in pitch and she gestured wildly. She shook me roughly by the shoulder to get my attention and I turned my head.

She sighed and shuffled off in disgust.

The event leading up to my eventual collapse in the armchair still pushed inward, jagged edges that pierced my oblivion.

After leaving Will Holmes, I'd driven back to the office and attempted to read through the records for the two other murders, before I'd given up and decided to go home. I'd put on some music, the guitar riffs of Muse easing me into another bender of drinking and pacing until I gave up pondering and sank into my old faithful chair.

Somehow, I still held a deluded belief that the memory of Jessica Holmes' s crime scene would leave me once I did get some sleep. They say insanity is doing the same thing over and over and expecting a different result, but based on my lack of evidence, self-deception was all I had.

I'd begun drinking again over the last week, and now the floodgates were opened, there was nothing else for it but to continue. Unfortunately, now I'd re-acquired my taste for it, it seemed it had lost its full anaesthetic effect, although it took the edges off the memories.

Sometimes.

"This is unbelievable, Jack; your kids need you. I need you. I thought your drinking days were over a long time ago?" Abbie had obviously headed back to bed, thought better of it and returned for round two.

"Look. Give me a break. I'm investigating the torture, rape and murder of a seven-year-old girl." I said. I didn't expect sympathy, but I least hoped she would cut me a break and leave me to my own devices for a while.

"Your kids need you, Jack; they are still young. You'll never get this time back."

"So they say."

She blew out air from between her teeth. "They say it for a reason. The girls won't be this age for long Jack, enjoy this time with them while you can. You're ignoring your own kids for the sake of one who's dead. I know you're committed to the job, but you made a commitment to us too, remember?"

I didn't have an answer for her, or, not one that she'd be satisfied with, so I said nothing.

"I understand this is a horrible case. I can't imagine what that's like but the drinking is just making it all worse, including the nightmares. I heard you scream again last night." I vaguely recalled her hand on my arm when I'd sat up bolt upright, my breath coming hard and fast, although I didn't recall screaming until the exact moment the screams woke me too. Instead, I'd padded downstairs, back to the music, and my old bottle of familiar comfort.

"Look, I just need some time. I'll solve it soon. I have to; just bear with me for a bit longer. For better or worse, remember?" I said, grabbing a bottle and pushing myself up to sit in the chair a little higher.

"It's more *worse* than *better*, at this moment in time." Abbie's gaze didn't falter. "And for God's sake, have a shower. You don't smell good,"

I needed to get up. There was nothing else for it but a trip to the bathroom which meant maybe I could wash off the stain of this case. I leaned forward in the chair, and she stormed off in disgust.

I would never admit it to Abbie, but I knew I was on a slippery slope. I had been kidding myself that I could stop drinking anytime, and it was a pretty lie—pure and simple.

If I was having a tough time of it now, I wasn't sure how I would go as the investigation progressed. Things would only get worse from here, with it ramping up in intensity the more it unravelled. I had told Abbie to back off and give me some breathing space, but as the nightmares and the far-too-frequent returns to armchair drinking showed, I wondered if I'd solve it. Instead—at least for now—

I was just collecting cobwebs and pondering on the evidence, the lot of an embittered detective.

I climbed the stairs and headed for the bathroom.

I thought about the crime scene photos and the timeline I'd constructed so far, as well as the other two murders I'd discovered which instinct had told me was related to this one. I didn't have the evidence yet, but knew deep in my bones this was the work of a serial killer. The files I'd begun reading for the two other murders, claimed Taylor Wentworth and Bianca Baker were most likely murdered by Dean Brown, convicted for rape and murder, later killed by a drug dealer a few weeks earlier. A now retired homicide detective David Wilson, had noted his conclusions but stated that due to lack of evidence (including no DNA match and a reluctance on the part of the prosecutor to gain a conviction) the jobs were both to be shifted to open and unsolved until further evidence became available.

I'd tried getting in touch with David Wilson, but apparently he was overseas.

I turned on the shower, the warmth spreading through my skin, and I groaned, beginning to relax. I wondered if DS Rae Swanson would call me back.

There weren't that many murders in the Knox area, especially not of young children. But in the last few months, there'd been two earlier murders of young children, girls of similar age with the same haunting blonde hair. No way was it pure coincidence.

I turned off the shower taps and dried myself with a bright red towel. I yanked my bathrobe off the hook, wrapped it around myself and headed back downstairs. As I had expected, Abbie had given up on me and retreated upstairs to check on the girls, conceding defeat and probably collapsing into our bed to try and sleep.

I headed back to what had become my late-night cave, grabbing the remote and turning the TV on. I pushed the button down hard to turn the volume of the late show down low, and decided that rather than listen to the host's drivel, I'd go hunting in the kitchen and find something to eat.

As I rummaged through the contents of the refrigerator, my phone buzzed and vibrated across the kitchen table. I raced over to it to see who called me at this late hour. I smiled. DS Rae Swanson had finally decided to return my call.

I pressed the green button and pulled the phone to my ear.

"Jack Fletcher," I said. Although I guessed it was near midnight, I decided to answer with my standard greeting.

"Jack? I thought I'd get voice mail. Sorry it's taken a while to get back to you, I've been busy. You know how that goes."

"Yeah," I said, wishing she'd get to the point and give me the information I needed.

"My name is DS Rae Swanson. You left a message about possibly similar jobs to two I referred to you guys?" she said. Her voice sounded husky; maybe she too had enjoyed one too many whiskeys in her time.

"Thanks for calling me back. Yes, I'm interested in your impressions in the murders of Taylor Wentworth and Bianca Baker, two little girls. There's been another murder of a child, a young girl, and I'm wondering if the murders are linked. Same hair colour, age... Let's be honest, there aren't that many children of a similar age in this area." I said.

"Possibly," she said, although she didn't sound convinced. "Another girl is missing, currently with missing persons." I needed a meeting with her. It would be hell of a lot easier to convince her face-to-face than over the telephone.

"Could we meet?" I said. "I wanted to run through the similarities, and it would be better face to face than over the phone."

I paused, daring her to respond and hardly daring to breathe. If Swanson wasn't convinced, it would prove that much more difficult to wrap up the Jessica Holmes case.

"I'm over on the other side of the city at the moment," she said. "Can you give me a call in the morning?. I'm pretty sure I'm coming out that way tomorrow."

Detective Swanson seemed fairly genuine, but if she was putting me off, she wouldn't get far. I could be like a dog with a bone when I wanted to.

"Okay will do" I said. I really didn't care if I sounded desperate, I just needed an end to the spiral of drinking, wishing, pondering and all too real nightmares.

I hung up. I went hunting for another bottle of whiskey, padded back to my brown worn armchair, made myself comfortable, and leaned back in it. I was all out of whiskey.

I turned up the sound on the late-night show, but it barely dented my melancholia.

My phone pinged to alert me to a text message.

It was the Team Leader, Selena, probably to remind me of my press duties the following day. Like most cops, this was one of those duties I'd rather be tossed off a cliff than agree to do, but then most of us had a love/hate, primarily annoying relationship with the press, a necessary evil.

Not that Selena cared much; she just needed the job done and it was my case, irrespective of whether I liked it or not. I needed to be up early the next morning. No more scotch for me that night.

She wanted me to speak at a press conference the next day and the media unit would arrive to brief me on my story beforehand. Great.

Press conferences were always a double-edged sword. None of the cops I spoke to liked being the centre of attention, but they did the trick as far as tips and calls from the public were concerned. It meant we got calls pestering us for a sound bite, a slick sounding quote, but we deflected as required and worked with the Media Unit as needed. They'd be pushing me to prepare a smooth briefing for the public. Maybe it would do the trick. The high percentage of calls from Crimestoppers usually went nowhere, but just sometimes, a tip became a real lead, and at the moment, I was information-hungry.

I sighed and sat back in the chair. I closed my eyes, a vain attempt to get some sleep. A press conference first thing Wednesday. Great.

CHAPTER SEVEN

I PARKED MY CAR AND arrived at the office just after 8 o'clock the next morning. I'd decided eventually to call it a night, finished with the whiskey by 1 a.m. and managed a few hours' sleep compared to zero the night before.

Jerry Wallace called out as I hung my jacket over the back of the chair, dropped my wallet and keys on the desk and sighed as I sat down.

"Hey, superstar. Looking forward to your press conference today?" Wallace said with a grin.

"Funny guy," I said. "Is the boss around?"

"She was here a couple minutes ago. Check the kitchen, she's usually getting into the coffee by now." Wallace turned back to his screen.

Hicks had demanded I lead the press conference, but the twist in my gut told me she'd done so only because of the rough time this job had brought me. And if there was one thing I didn't need or want, it was sympathy—sweet and warm until you woke up cold and wet. Never the top of my list as far as emotions went.

I figured I'd need to make the obligatory rumblings about not wanting to do it, but the media unit would arrive soon, and my chances of backing out were slim. What I didn't understand was why she chose this job to shove me into the spotlight? Was it my run-in with the journalist at the crime scene? Had someone told her I'd thrown up in the bathroom?

Heat rose in my face. I sure as hell hoped not; the squad room had been empty when I'd checked, although I'd been in a hurry, so Garrett or Jerry Wallace might have been obscured behind a short cubicle wall, but then they didn't seem the type to squeal.

A door slammed behind me, and I turned. Hicks gestured with her chin, mid-stride on the way to her office, and I followed. Hicks sat down, leaned back and lifted her head. Her office contained an old spider plant, brown at the end of the leaves, an old filing cabinet heaving with the burden of piles of paperwork, and her desk that gave only the occasional glimmer of a surface underneath. A picture of her teenage daughter was propped against a pen holder underneath her screen.

"Fletcher, you grace us with your presence," she said. Although her hair hung across her face, I thought I saw the ghost of a wry smile.

I didn't take up her snarky comment, as the lack of sleep and pile of empty bottles forming beside my old armchair at home hadn't exactly lifted my mood, and any reply would only lead to a fast road to nowhere. It was a verbal jousting I was in no mood for.

"I came about the press conference," I said quietly, shoving both hands into the pockets of my pants.

Boss lady turned in her chair. "Oh, yeah. Looking forward to your media mentor? Tracey should be here in about—" She lifted her silver, gentlemans Seiko watch far too close to her eyes—"ten minutes.... Early start, she said."

God damn it, she loved to rub it in.

"Come on, Selena," I said pulling my hands out of my jean's pockets. "You know I'm hands-on. I get out and knock on doors, press isn't exactly my specialty,"

Hicks rubbed at her chin. "No shit. I'm feeling generous, Jack. I've decided to put the press conference on hold for now, keep it up our sleeve. What we really need now are leads, so I've had Crimestoppers put out a bulletin on the news last night, based on Gemma's description of the suspect. I gave your details as the lead investigator."

I let out a breath. Hicks loved playing games, part of the years we'd worked together on and off. For now, I could do what I did best, and investigate the job. "Thanks," I said and turned towards the doorway to head back to my desk.

As I took a step forward and reached the doorway, she called out and I leaned my left hand against the frame, turning to look at her.

"Before you go, Jack," I didn't like the quiet warning tone in her voice. "Don't get too cocky; you're not off the hook yet."

"Cocky? Me?"

She deliberately ignored me. "At some point, you'll need to learn to play nice with the media unit; they'll be in contact today to help you form a story. When I do call a press conference, you'll be speaking. It'll be good for you to field questions. The media's not exactly at the top of my Christmas card list either, but we need them, and it'd pay for you to remember that." She picked up her pen and resumed underlining some important point in her paperwork.

I walked back down the corridor towards my desk, sat down, slumped forward and gazed at the monitor for some kind of epiphany. All I needed was one morsel, a frayed piece of string to pick at and unravel, an inkling of the monster's face, the worm that brutalised beautiful, blonde-haired Jessica Holmes.

I checked my email program, and two emails were highlighted. I clicked on the first one from the Forensics Lab.

DNA analysis for another job, I forwarded it to Wallace for now.

I clicked on the second one from Crimestoppers, which was pretty damn fast. Usually, the crazies rang up first, but the contents of the email indicated that this caller might be relatively sane and helpful rather than desperate for attention.

His name was Kevin Barnes. He claimed to recognise the man based on the description of the suspect, along with the vehicle details provided. Barnes had also listed his address and phone number; he lived only ten minutes away from the station.

My pulse picked up pace a little. I picked up the phone and dialled the number.

"Hello?" the voice sounded gravelly, possibly an older man.

"Kevin Barnes?" I said. "This is Detective Sergeant Jack Fletcher, of Melbourne Crime Command. You contacted Crimestoppers about the child murder case."

A pause. "A terrible business," he muttered. "I've seen that idiot at the park, and had my suspicions, so when I saw the description on the telly..."

"Mr. Barnes, do you mind if I drop by to talk to you? It's important. You're at home at the moment?"

"Yes, yes I am."

"I'll be there in about fifteen minutes," I said. Spurred on by the prospect of a possible lead in the case, I grabbed my jacket from the back of the chair, swiped my keys and wallet from the desk and headed out to the car park.

Unlocking the car, I plugged the address into the GPS, and reversed out.

My route would take me down the main four-lane freeway out of the central business district of Melbourne, the principal thoroughfare of Burwood Highway. Then, it would pass down Ferntree Gully Road, past the bustling shopping centre, and onto Ashton Road. The home of Kevin Barnes was situated on Blaise Court, a quiet no-through road in the middle-class suburbia of Ferntree Gully.

Surrounded by large trees, it looked like not a soul stirred at the brick veneer, double-fronted home. I parked my unmarked Ford Falcon on the narrow street out front, pushed down on the key remote and walked down the short driveway to the concrete front porch. Someone loved the house, obviously. The front porch was decked out with a quaint white painted bench, surrounded by tree ferns and many other plants.

The sturdy wooden front door opened as I reached out to press the doorbell. I couldn't see Kevin Barnes' face through the security door, but with the click of a lock, he had it open.

As I'd guessed from his voice, Kevin Barnes looked to be in his sixties, grey and balding, dressed smartly in navy dress pants and a dark pullover.

"Detective Fletcher, come in please." He gestured with one hand for me to enter the hallway, opening the door wide.

"Thank you." My shoes clacked on the shiny polished floorboards. I sat down on an armchair in a neat living room, with overstuffed couches and lace doilies perched underneath ornate ceramic figurines. The living room was the first on the right off a long hallway.

Sitting on an armchair directly opposite, he took a deep breath before speaking. "I almost wasn't going to call again, but I have grandchildren, and visit that park fairly regularly." He dropped his hands between his legs and stared at the floor for a moment. "Sorry, I didn't offer you anything. Can I get you a tea or coffee?"

"Thank you, I'm good for now."

"I wish I hadn't had to contact you but..."

Barnes hesitated.

"You were talking about visiting the park?" I wondered if there was a Mrs. Barnes, and if so, where she was? If Mrs. Barnes appeared, she might elbow her husband and prompt him to continue. I did often find the older witnesses rambled on a bit, as if it was a social call.

"Oh yes, sorry. It's all so disturbing, I suppose I've been trying not to think about it, then that Crimestoppers thing on the telly brought it all back. Yes, the man's at that park quite a bit. I've seen him a few times, and there was just something about him that wasn't quite right."

"In what way?" I said after a pause in the conversation, where I took out a notebook and pen to take a few notes.

"Well, for a start, he never had children with him, so I guess he wasn't a father, but he seemed a bit too interested in the kids, calling them over. I saw the red truck and overheard him asking some of the children if they'd like to come and see the puppies he had. That set my alarm bells off straight away." Barnes sighed and rubbed his chin.

I decided to stay quiet, attempting to encourage him to talk with an, "Mm, hm." Then, I leaned back in the chair and waited, my pen paused over the notebook.

Barnes cleared his throat. "He even approached my grandkids, which was the final straw. I approached him and asked his name. He didn't want to give it at first, until I glanced at his vehicle registration, wrote it down and asked why he seemed to be at the park so often when he didn't have kids in tow. He gave me a foul look and turned away to get back in the car. Never did answer me. I thought I'd scared him away from the park, but obviously, he came back."

I breathed out slowly. "And when was that, the time you spoke to him, Kevin?"

"About a week ago, maybe longer. I did call at the time, but never heard back. So I called again."

I recoiled. That was right around the time Jessica went missing. "You called before?"

"I did yes"

"Do you remember who you spoke to?"

"Sorry I don't"

"Okay, I'll see what I can find out. I don't suppose you wrote down the registration details? Do you still have them?"

"Yeah. I do." Barnes smiled, sure of himself as he sat back in the armchair. "I kept them in the kitchen drawer just in case I might ever need them. Then I saw the description on the news last night, and my blood turned cold. I wonder if I should have followed up more, although the guy did drive away after

I'd made my note. I guess I wasn't intimidating enough." He dropped his head.

"You did the right thing." Finally, I had a scumbag in the area, a place to start. "If you could get those details, that would be really helpful," I said. "Do you remember his name?"

"I'll never forget it. Marlin Jones. An unusual name. Hang on a minute, I'll go find the bit of paper where I wrote it down; won't be long." He pushed his hands down on his thighs, levered himself up, and walked out of the room.

Marlin Jones. Maybe this creep could lead me to the killer, or maybe the killer was Marlin Jones himself. I'd also be interested in who took Barnes call, and then promptly ignored it. Either way, I'd have a talk to Jones about why he hung around children's parks and playgrounds.

Kevin arrived back to the living area with a crumpled piece of paper in his hands. "Here it is," he said, and handed it to me, chest out. "He definitely has the vehicle you're looking for. I'm surprised he went back to the park, considering I saw him and talked to him, and remember what he looks like."

I took the piece of paper from him, and rubbed at a corner with my thumb, before folding it and tucking it into a compartment within the notebook. "Thank you, you did the right thing." Barnes stared at me, the colour drained from his face.

"Don't be too hard on yourself; you could have just let him go, but you relied on your instincts. Unfortunately, with characters like these, deterrents and warnings aren't usually enough. I'll pay him a visit and find out what's going on."

Barnes stood up, brushing down his pants and taking a deep breath. "The thing is, that little girl that was taken from the park, that could have been one of my grandchildren. It worries me that people like this are out there, hanging around parks and kids' play areas."

I walked slowly back towards the front door. Barnes opened it and paused in the hallway. I reached out and shook his hand. "I'll be in touch. The information has really helped. Thanks again."

Barnes murmured quietly, and I headed back towards my car. I intended to get back to my desk and look up Marlin Jones to find out where he lived and follow up. I unlocked the car, got in, and started it up.

The drive was short, and for a moment, the sun shone brightly.

I thought more about Jones. I'd need to keep myself in check with him; I'd already been pulled into line over the argument with the journalist, so another outburst and Hicks would be forced into a situation where she'd need do something a bit more drastic and risk the problem falling back onto her.

Staying calm in the face of a sadistic paedophile didn't come easily, but I'd do it. I arrived back at the station, and although I didn't think it was all that easy to read me, Jerry Wallace looked up and smiled as I arrived back at my desk. "Got a new lead then, huh?"

"Something like that," I mumbled as I threw my jacket on the empty desk beside me and dropped my wallet and keys into a desk drawer.

I opened my notebook, removed the piece of paper Barnes had given me and clicked on the mouse to activate the computer. *I'm coming for you, Marlin Jones, ready or not.*

I opened the VicRoads program, and typed in the vehicle registration details. Details for Marlin Jones flashed up on the screen after a few seconds. I sucked in a breath and stared, unable to move.

"Of all the nerve," I whispered.

Marlin Jones lived on the same street as the Holmes family.

CHAPTER EIGHT

I SAT IN THE CAR OUTSIDE the home of Marlin Jones for a minute, trying to compose myself before I knocked on the front door. It looked exactly as I'd imagined it; a rundown old home with green peeling paint on the exterior and fence, overgrown weeds surrounding a rusted old car dumped in the front yard.

My right hand paused over the key, ready to pull it out of the ignition. I closed my eyes, took a breath, and removed it. I'd need to keep my cool with this guy, no matter how much I wanted to cause him pain, the same pain he'd quite possibly given the Holmes family.

I got out of the car, closed the car door and locked it. I stood on the footpath outside, waiting for some sign that he had seen me, the twitching of curtains or the opening of a door.

Nothing.

I walked towards the gate, pushing it with my knee until eventually it gave way and swung open with force, banging back against the short brick wall. I looked around at the tiny garden, its grass knee-high. The place looked like a drug den, little to no maintenance work done, and no care for the house whatsoever. I headed up to the rotten wooden porch, walking carefully up the steps. I knocked on the frame of the faded security door with its red paint worn off, took a step back, and waited.

After about a minute, I reached forward to knock again, when I heard movement inside. The door opened. There was next to no light inside what looked to be a dingy hallway. In front of me stood a man whose mere appearance repulsed me, almost reptilian in appearance, and looking very much like the stereotypical paedophile. Acne scars dotting across his cheeks also made me think he was using hard drugs. Thin, red-haired and possibly in his forties, the guy chewed gum loudly. He hadn't shaved in a few days.

"Marlin Jones?" I said.

"Who's asking?" he replied, leaning against the doorway.

I flashed my badge. "Detective Sergeant Jack Fletcher, Melbourne Homicide, got a few questions."

Jones' eyes widened, and he tried to push the door closed, but he wasn't quick enough. I hoped to hell he didn't run, I wasn't in the mood for a foot pursuit. I shoved my boot inside the door frame and jammed it open. The bastard kept trying to push it closed.

"Open the door."

"Got a warrant?"

"Do I need one?" I said through gritted teeth.

Jones gloated for a second too long, and I pushed harder, shuffling closer towards the doorway before he relented and opened the door a little.

"DO YOU VISIT THE LOCAL park often? You know, the one where little girls hang out?"

"What are you trying to say?"

"What are you not saying?"

"Nothing, I don't like cops turning up asking questions that's all."

"The only people that don't like cops asking questions, are ones that have something to hide." My skin crawled and I brushed my right hand down my left forearm.

"I don't think I like your tone." My chest burned. If Jones was trying to irritate me, his methods were working so far. I took a deep breath, dropping my shoulders.

"Too bad," I said.

"Look, what's this all about?"

"The murder of a little girl." I fumbled in my pocket for a picture of Jessica Holmes. "Know anything about this girl?" I shoved the picture inches from his face and watched as he flinched.

"Of course, I don't. What is this?" Jones stared at the floor.

"This is a child murder enquiry, one I think you know more about than you're telling." Jones didn't look up.

I thought about the crime scene, about the body of Jessica Holmes alone in Sherbrooke National Park, about the cuts and burns littered across her torso. Rather than stare at Jones, I fixed my gaze on the wall beside him, and worked on carefully controlling my voice and tone. "Jessica Holmes was found brutalised, tortured and raped, and then dumped in a forest like garbage. She played in the park nearby, and witnesses mentioned they saw you speaking to her the day she went missing.

Are you still going to tell me you don't know anything about this?"

"No, I can't help you." Jones stared at me, his face covered in a thin film of sweat. I couldn't help feeling this man's dirty appearance probably reflected a dirty, perverted mind.

"So, you've never spoken to Jessica Holmes? Please, look again at this picture to jog your memory." I hadn't lowered my hand and continued to hold her picture in front of Jones' nose. "Have you ever met this girl, spoken to her at the park?"

Jones paused, shifting his weight from one foot to the other. "Can't say I remember her. I can't help you."

Heat rose in my face, and I breathed slowly, attempting to control my anger. Marlin Jones wasn't about to admit to anything.

"Is that your vehicle parked in the driveway Mr. Jones?" I asked.

"Yes, it is."

"A witness placed you at the local park, standing beside that vehicle on the day Jessica Holmes went missing. You asked her if she'd like to come and see some puppies. Can you tell me about that?"

I dropped my hand and placed the photograph carefully back into my jacket pocket. I concentrated on keeping my tone calm, but the ache in the back of my throat, and the heat in my face weren't going anywhere.

"I'm sorry; I don't know what you're talking about."

"You're saying you weren't at the park, and you never met Jessica Holmes? Is that correct?" I said, keeping my voice low.

"That's right," said Marlin Jones. "Look, I have to go now."

"One last question before I leave. If I do a search against your name, will I find any criminal history? Crimes against children, child pornography, anything like that?"

Jones wouldn't look at me and let out a sigh. "Look, like I said, I really gotta go." I peered through the doorway attempting to get a look inside. "I'd like a quick look around before I go, if you don't mind," I said. I wanted to see how he lived, whether anything looked out of place, or anything locked away. But I knew my rights were very limited and had to hope he didn't know it.

I was going to be disappointed.

"If you want to look around my property, you'll need a search warrant," he said. This time, he met my gaze.

"I'm aware of that," I said quietly. "I wasn't suggesting I wanted to search the house, Mr. Jones. Just a quick look around."

He fixed my gaze with his own. "Same thing. Search warrant," he said, simply, and it seemed this was as far as we'd get that day.

I was close to getting a search warrant with what we had, in any case, only he didn't know it. Jones was damn lucky this was a friendly visit. For now. "Keep this in mind, Mr. Jones. If you're lying to me, and if you had anything to do with the disappearance and murder of Jessica Holmes, I will find out, and I will get a search warrant. That's a promise you can count on. Meanwhile, maybe you'd care to continue this little chat back at the station?"

Jones paled and cleared his throat. "I know my rights. Don't come around here threatening me. If you want me to come down to the station, I'll need some notice, so I can get legal help."

Shit. The bastard had clammed up again; he knew the law.

"You do that," I said. This time, I didn't bother to hide the growl in my voice but I moved away from the front door; he had made his views felt and it was time to leave. As soon as I backed away, Jones slammed the door shut. The bang echoed out through the street and curtains twitched in the house across the way.

I took a deep breath, and stepped down the rickety porch steps, pausing in the shabby garden. I stared up at the home of the man I believed had abducted Jessica Holmes. He'd retreated into the dark squalor, probably to plot his next move.

I made my way back to the car and got inside, taking a minute to think about what had just happened. Once there, I let out a sigh, driving down the street a way before stopping and turning up the stereo to drown out my silent scream. Once I'd done that, I headed back to the Melbourne Crime Command to look up Marlin Jones, determined one way or the other that I'd get him. And that included a search warrant.

After fighting traffic on the journey back to crime command, I arrived at my desk primed and ready. I'd worked with Jerry Wallace for years, and he must have picked up my mood when I sent my keys and wallet spinning across my desk. He spun in his office chair and looked at me.

"What the hell happened?"

"Marlin Jones, that's what."

"Oh yeah?" Wallace kept his cards close to his chest, revealing little about what went on beneath the skin; I guessed that was why we worked so well together.

"Jones was seen at the park with Jessie, it's him I'm sure of it." I let out a breath and sat down in the chair.

"He was there, with his red truck, scouting out kids, asking them if they wanted to come back and see his puppies. Classic line. Unbelievable."

"You went to his place? Get anything?" Wallace didn't move from his relaxed position, reclining back in his chair.

"Not much, said he knew nothing about it, never met Jessica. I mentioned witnesses had seen him talking to her, still nothing." Heat rose in my face at the thought of the weasel feigning his innocence.

"Got under your skin huh?"

"You could say that. I invited him back to the station, and he refused, claiming he'd need to make a phone call and get legal advice."

"He got a record?"

"I was just about to check that. All I want is one good reason to turn his place inside out." Wallace had already turned back to his desk and clicked open the program to do a search.

"Marlin Jones, you said? Got a date of birth?"

I reached across and went through paperwork on my desk, until I got the printout of the search I'd run on his vehicle registration details.

"Yeah." I got up and walked across to stand beside Wallace as he entered Marlin Jones' date of birth into the system.

It took a few seconds, then it appeared on the screen clear as day.

Jones had a record all right. I swallowed, hard. Wallace whistled. "Well what do you know, Mr. Innocence has a record for sex with a minor, more than ten years ago." He looked up at me, and I stared back.

"No wonder he was so cagey. Claimed he didn't know Jessica, never went to the park, never met her, even though a couple of witnesses placed him there."

"Nothing surprises me anymore when it comes to rock spiders." Most of us in law enforcement used the inside term for paedophiles.

"Better get moving, Jerry. I'll get started on a search warrant application. Can't wait to toss his place while he watches."

Marlin Jones so far was the prime suspect, but I had zero in the way of evidence linking Jones to the crime.

I needed to get that search warrant ready and submitted to the court.

CHAPTER NINE

BRIGHT LIGHT FILTERED through the clouds. The windows were high up in my cubicle and covered with grey vertical blinds. The quietness covered me like a blanket.

I shifted in my office chair, pulling it towards the screen. I knew Marlin Jones was our guy. All I needed now was some evidence to put him away. I powered up the computer, opening the template for a search warrant and starting to fill it in to get it submitted. I began madly pecking at the keyboard, chewing my lip.

If there was one thing cops didn't talk about, it was paperwork. Most members of the public had no idea how much administration and bureaucracy were involved in solving a crime, the less glamorous side of an investigation.

In this case though, I had to make sure I did everything right, even if it took time. The last thing I wanted was the case getting tossed out on appeal due to some minor technicality.

I got on a roll, developed a second wind as I filled in the final fields of the warrant request. I took a breath, lifted my fingers from the keyboard and leaned back, pushing away from the desk. I felt a presence next to me. I looked up to my right where Selena Hicks frowned down on me, arms crossed.

"I've got top brass breathing down my neck. What's the latest?"

"Got a subspecies; he has a record as a sex offender but I'm going to need a search warrant."

"Okay, expedite it. Media unit will be here shortly. Play nice, okay?"

I let out a sigh and stood up, shoving my hands in my pockets. "Always." I lifted my head. "Let me guess, they're going to coach me, so I can play nice at the press conference?"

"You catch on quick. Tracey from the media unit will be here in..." Hicks checked her watch. "Any minute now. You're best placed to answer questions anyway. It'll be fine. Tracey will coach you on your responses."

Great. Now I had to go through the information I had and refresh my memory. Not that we had many facts to begin with; we were shit out of luck.

Hicks left, and I turned back to my screen. I finished off the search warrant and emailed it through.

For now, I'd need to wait.

I sifted through a folder of paperwork, the information I had at hand, before the boss lady appeared again, leaning one elbow against the short divider.

"This is a task force now, Jack. Project Beacon, you know that, right?"

"Yeah."

I figured as much; anything involving children, sexual predators and serial killers usually became a task force. And since the media were all over it, more resources would be allocated along with more dealings with the media. The community would be up in arms about it, in some cases staging peaceful protests until the killer was found.

Hicks' phone beeped. "Tracey Reynolds is here. She'll be out at reception shortly,"

"Okay." I didn't look up from my paperwork.

"Ready for your big moment?"

"Yeah," I said, getting up from my seat. Hicks smiled.

"These people are professionals, Jack; give them a chance."

"I got nothing, no evidence, a possible suspect but nothing tying him to the crime. I don't think I'm exactly going to instill confidence in the public." I shoved my hands in my pockets and walked to reception.

A short woman with slicked-back blond hair walked through the sliding doors. Reception was empty, so the woman looked straight at me.

"I'm here to see DS Fletcher. Tracey Reynolds, Media Unit,"

"DS Fletcher."

She handed me a card. "Conference room?" she asked.

"Follow me."

The conference room was on the next level up. We were the only people in the lift.

"We'll need at least an hour." Her voice was light and quiet, surprising given she worked in the media unit.

"I'm not sure what I can say." I cleared my throat

"The general public is scared; it's high profile. There's public interest in the Holmes murder. That park and the playground are deserted now. They need reassurance, that's all," said Reynolds.

"I don't know if I can give them that," I said quietly. "I don't have a whole lot, it's still early days."

We exited the lift and headed for the conference room. I paused, resting a hand on the door handle and looked at her.

She gestured with her palm out. "Let's go in and get started; we can run through a few scenarios."

I opened the door for her, following behind her and taking a seat at the conference table. I paused for a moment, taking in the quiet, letting it wash over me. I gazed around to get my bearings, taking in the large windows behind Tracey who sat straight in the chair. She grabbed a black diary tucked under her arm and took hold of a pen from inside it.

"Okay. I've been briefed. I recommend you start with something like explaining we have a person of interest, then thank the public for the leads provided after the Crimestoppers bulletin, and let them know the investigation is progressing"

"What about question time? Judging by the interest early on, this will be a circus."

"It usually is, but prior planning will help. How about you start with what you know so far? No names, of course. Run through it now with me. Give it a dry run."

I began, fumbling at first, but Tracey let me go, trying to get it straight. I gave her a rundown, the crime scene—minus my reaction—the Holmes marital separation, the family reaction, and the progress on the case so far. Tracey barely reacted, a true professional.

"It's a fine line, but ultimately we need the media for help. Keep it professional, maintain confidentiality and you'll be fine."

"But, public speaking..." One good thing about being a cop was that initially, it had meant keeping a low profile on social media and otherwise. At this point in my career, the reverse was true. I wasn't sure I liked it.

Tracey shuffled some papers. "Yes, there's that. But the media attention can help you solve the case and get them off your back."

"Okay."

"You'll be fine. You're a dedicated detective. Focus on that, on the family, getting the results and the rest will fall into place."

Unconvinced, I nodded.

"I'll be at the conference. I'll speak first and introduce you. I'll let you answer as many questions as you can but if you lose confidence, give me a nod and I'll step in."

I wanted to get back to my desk, make some calls, get out on the street and talk to people, but for now I'd need to take the pain. I checked my phone. Text from Hicks.

Press conference 1pm in conference room.

Tracey stared at her phone. "I might grab a coffee. Not long until it starts."

As I walked back to the second floor kitchen to grab a coffee, through the frosted glass I saw a crowd forming in the corridor, most likely journalists.

I didn't want to see them so I took the lift downstairs and headed back to my office. Jerry Wallace sat on his office chair, while Collen perched on the corner of his desk. I walked over and stood between them. Wallace looked at me, Collen didn't.

"Got the shits, mate?" Wallace peered up at me.

I didn't answer.

"Could be worse. At least this way, your kids get to see you."

"Fuck off."

"I would, but unfortunately I get paid to hang around the joint. Find bad guys."

I walked away. Tracey Reynolds intercepted me on the way to the bathroom. "Okay, Jack, we'll need to go back up shortly. I'll introduce you, and Selena will be there too. You ready?"

"As ready as I'll ever be."

"Come through," she said, then walked down the corridor and we took the lift as we as we talked. In a minute or two I found myself in front of the conference room beside her.

Tracey opened the door, and I saw the room was half full of journalists, with twenty minutes to go until the conference. Ted Richards chatted with a photographer in the corner. Hicks entered the room behind me.

"Leave him to me, Fletcher," said Tracey Reynolds, her voice low and quiet.

As we walked across the room, I saw the change in Reynolds' demeanour. Her shoulders back, she plastered a smile across her face and extended a hand to the journalist. "Ted, glad you could make it."

Ted Richards smiled back. "Thanks for inviting me. So, I take it I'm permitted to ask questions today? Otherwise, this is going to be a—"

"Call me Tracey, please. Of course, all your questions are welcomed," she said, smiling again so hard that I wondered if her face hurt. "You know," she went on, "I'm sorry if we were unable to help you with a story earlier, but... protocols, you know. Nothing personal, and we're glad you're here." She smiled again.

"Will you be holding the press conference yourself?" said Richards, flicking a furtive glance in my direction.

"Actually, Detective Fletcher will be running the conference, as he's the current lead on the case. I'm hoping we can put the past behind us, Mr. Richards," she said, staring right at him. "We're all on the same team, wanting justice for the victim. And you're a big part of us getting that."

"I think we can forget what's past," Richards said, the smile still fixed on his face.

"I appreciate it. Now, if you'll excuse us, we need to prepare." We both walked toward the podium, set upon a small platform area. I stuffed my hands in my pockets in an attempt to calm my nerves. I needed a drink. Selena Hicks was behind the podium, hidden in an area partially blocked out from the lights with dark blockout fabric.

"You'll be fine, Fletcher; you know the case, and the family, just be yourself." Hicks nudged me gently up onto the podium.

Somehow, that didn't seem like it would be enough.

Reynolds stepped forward. "In a minute, I'll get up to the podium and introduce you. Remember, we want to reassure the public about the safety of our public parks and playgrounds, and let them know we do have a person of interest, okay?"

She smiled at me and approached the podium. When did she become so relaxed about the process? I envied her calmness.

She cleared her throat. "Ladies and gentlemen, thank you for your attendance today. If you'll take your seats, we'll have some information for you regarding events as they stand. Thank you."

Reynolds waited patiently while they found their seats, and the murmuring subsided. I recognised some of the journalists, but others were completely new faces, eager for a story.

"Thank you for being here today. I'd like to introduce you the lead detective, who will brief you on developments in the murder of seven-year-old Jessica Holmes. If you could hold your questions until the end of the briefing, that would be appreciated. For now, I'll introduce the lead investigator on the case, Detective Sergeant Jack Fletcher." Reynolds finished, and after taking a deep breath, I moved to stand before the podium.

I cleared my throat. The room became silent, and I paused for a moment to compose myself. "My name is DS Jack Fletcher based at Melbourne Crime Command. We are currently investigating a heinous crime, the torture and murder of a seven-year-old child, Jessica Holmes. As you can imagine, her family is grieving and asks that you respect their privacy at this time. Please be assured, we are following up all leads, and we do have a person of interest. I would like to assure the public that Victoria Police has dedicated the resources needed to apprehend the perpetrator, and we would also like to thank them for their assistance so far." I managed to let out a breath, placed my hands on either side of the podium and waited.

A barrage of hands rose in the air. I chose what looked to be a female hand, closest to the front, and gestured in their direction.

"Yes," I said, and waited.

"Debbie McDonald, Five News. Given the nature of the crime, parents are fearful for their children playing in public parks. Do you have the suspect in custody? What can you tell us about the investigation?"

I knew we had next to nothing, but needed to make it sound palatable. My stomach churned. "All parents need to be vigilant rather than afraid. That means supervising children, whether that be in public playgrounds, parks, walking to school, or at any other public area. Vigilance is one of the best safeguards." I paused for a moment and took a breath. I'd surprised myself; my statement seemed to come from nowhere, but sounded reasonable, reassuring, logical. I continued. "In regard to a suspect, obviously I can't give away too much detail about an ongoing investigation, but we do have a person of interest, and are following up all lines of enquiry. I'd like to take this opportunity to thank the public for calling Crimestoppers. Their information has been invaluable."

Debbie McDonald nodded, and I moved on to the next question. I focused on the hands up in the first two rows and chose one at random. "Yes? Next question? Thank you"

The person stood up, and the blood drained from my face as I realised it was Ted Richards, who must have switched places and was now sitting in the front row.

"Given the nature of the murder, there has been some speculation that the murderer has done this before. Are you treating this as the work of a serial killer, and if so, is he still at large?" Richards met my gaze before taking his seat.

I cleared my throat and did my best to answer the question. "Given that it has been only 24 hours since Jessica was found, we are considering all options, and pursuing several leads, including the person of interest. As I stated earlier, the best defence against this type of perpetrator is keeping an eye out for suspicious behaviour and calling Crimestoppers. Once more information comes to light, I'll be able to advise further." Not really my best answer, but then I hadn't fully finalised my political skills in appearing to answer the question without really doing anything of the sort. I didn't dare turn around to see how Hicks had reacted.

"So, is that a *yes*? This could be the work of a serial killer?" Ted pushed the matter further.

"We can't comment at this stage, at least not until our investigation has concluded, although—again—we are grateful for the information we receive on the Crimestoppers line and strongly urge the public to continue to call." The words came from somewhere else, a place I didn't know existed.

My gut twisted, and the heat in my face continued to burn. It was obvious to me we had no idea what we were doing and bumbling through a press conference was not at the top of my to-do list. I'd made a complete mess of the whole thing.

"Thank you, Detective Fletcher," said Richards, scribbling furiously on a notepad.

Although I wanted to end the press conference there and then, I figured I'd need to take at least a couple more questions. I chose another hand from the back of the pack this time. "Yes?" I said.

"Kerryn Daniels, Channel Twelve. Can you tell us how the Holmes family are doing and has the possibility been considered that someone known to them murdered Jessica?" she said.

If I'd thought this one was easier to answer, I was kidding myself. I gripped the side of the podium tightly with both hands. Surely this would all be over soon.

"The Holmes family are doing as well as can be expected in this situation. Again, they request that their privacy be respected while they grieve for Jessica. Furthermore, as I mentioned earlier, we are following up on each and every line of enquiry, wherever that may lead, but we are still at the early stages of the investigation. We'll keep you updated as the case develops."

The reporter gave a thin smile and rested her pen on the notepad balancing on her knee. I waited a moment before choosing the next question, taking a moment to assess the mood.

The podium was brightly lit, and the rest of the room in dimmed lighting, so it took a few seconds to try and make out faces in the crowd. Judging by the number of hands still in the air, I could answer questions for the next couple of hours and still wouldn't get through them all.

I needed a couple of brownie points up my sleeve with Hicks, so I soldiered on, determined to do my best, no matter how pathetic my answers may be. It felt like we had nothing, no evidence, no answers, no clue. And the reason for that was because I wanted Marlin Jones badly, but evidence to arrest him was thin on the ground.

"Yes?" I said quietly, pointing at another hand.

"Thank you, Jarrod Reeves, Thirteen News. So, you don't have a suspect in custody? When do you anticipate an arrest will be made?"

My chest tightened, and the internal heat returned. "As I said earlier, we're still in the early stages of the investigation, but we have a person of interest. This is due largely to the public's response to the Crimestoppers bulletin, which we urge them to continue with. We treat all calls seriously and we do follow them up."

I breathed deeply, and turned to my right, where Hicks had appeared. Could the damn press conference get any worse?

Hicks shot me a piercing look and leaned towards the podium. I took a step back, and my knees buckled slightly, so I locked them into place.

Boss lady leaned over to the microphone. "I do apologise, but we will need to bring the press conference to a close I'm afraid, as there's been some urgent developments which we'll update you on as soon as we're able. For now, please direct all further questions to Tracey Reynolds in the Media Unit. Thank you."

As Tracey Reynolds reached the podium, I followed Hicks off the stage, the audience hum fading into the background. Hicks strode to the back corner of the room, turned and shoved her back against the wall. She stuffed both hands in her pockets.

"Another body's been found. A little girl, seven years old. Same location, Sherbrooke National Park. A stabbing."

CHAPTER TEN

AS PART OF PROJECT Beacon, Hicks had set up an alert on any similar cases involving young children. This job had been called in, and forensics were likely already at the scene. A few more detectives were getting called out.

I wanted to compare notes again with the detective I'd called earlier DS Swanson. Hicks had given me the woman's details. And there they were again: Detective Segeant Rae Swanson, out of the Ringwood/Maroondah station.

We'd spoken very briefly yesterday, and she'd mentioned a possible a call-back this morning on Jessica's case.

Swanson had been investigating the disappearance of another young girl, but 'her' little one had been missing for longer than Jessica was, almost three weeks before a body had shown up. Worse still, it seemed she'd been killed only towards the end of the missing period. Now, two months had elapsed since the discovery.

I wondered why he'd taken longer to murder that one? If these cases were related, that meant he'd kept Jessica Holmes for only four days before killing her.

Although evidence-wise there wasn't enough information to prove a relationship between the murders, this was the same killer, the same scumbag. It had to be. I knew it, felt it in my bones, wanting to catch him so bad I could taste it. I wanted to get the faceless killer out of my head and into a jail cell.

I'd do whatever it took to prove it and lock him up. This killer was male, not female, I figured, since cases of female child abusers and serial killers were rare.

SO FAR, I WAS IN ON the new job—murdered girl number four—as part of the task force, although technically it was murder number two, so I pulled out my mobile phone and called the number for Rae Swanson again, out at Maroondah Homicide. It was roughly 9pm. The number rang, then skipped a couple of beats.

"Maroondah CID." I recognised Harry Filsche, again. Swanson must have diverted her mobile to the front desk of Knox CID for some reason. Probably because Knox was 24 hours, while Maroondah, or Ringwood, was not.

"Hey, Harry, how's it going?"

"Jack."

"Boss told me there's a new job. A kid murdered again?"

A beat, a pause. "Yeah, little girl. Tough one."

Filsche had been in the job a long time, at least forty years I guessed, being close to retirement. But cases like this could crack the most hardened cops, including Filsche.

"Who found her?" I said.

"Couple of hikers walking through Sherbrooke Forest."

"At night?"

"Yeah well, not far from a known spot for romantics. Decided to take their love outside," Harry said.

"I'm in on this one, but I'm also looking for similarities to another case, little girl about the same age. Found in Sherbrooke Forest but a different part. Her name was Jessica Holmes, you called me on it?"

"Yeah, that's right. This girl was found in a creek. I'll send you the GPS details and a map. She's on the opposite side of the forest to where your girl was found. Might need your hiking boots."

"What else can you tell me?"

"Uniform's secured the scene. Forensics are on the way, called out maybe half an hour ago; won't be long." Harry cleared his throat. "He stabbed her. I just hope she went in peace. DS Swanson will know more."

"Get her to call me, will you?"

"Sure thing. I'll send her a text. She'll want to nail this bastard." said Filsche

"Don't we all, Jack. I'll message you the details like I said. Hope you nail the son of a bitch."

"Yeah, me too. Thanks Harry," I said and hung up.

Most people familiar with Sherbrooke National Park knew it was massive. 87,000 acres. I'd need the name of the creek and the nearest access point. Just as well I had my boots in the car; it was time to do some hiking and get to the scene.

Most of the others had left, and the press was gone, only Hicks and Holmberg were hanging around. I walked away and gave Hicks a half-wave.

"Jack," she said, lifting up her head, and beckoning to me. I walked the few steps back. Holmberg stood beside her, one foot against the wall, watching me.

"Easy on this one. I get it, it's rough, it's a kid. If you need time off, take it. There's already a detective on this one. You can talk to her tomorrow."

She eyed me, watching for some indication of a mental collapse. She wasn't getting it. Hicks's stare went right through me, and I wondered if she knew about the booze, the nightmares, the fights with Abbie.

"Look, I want this scumbag bad, we all do. I want in early, I'll talk to Swanson on the scene. I'll do whatever it takes to put him away."

"No, Jack, not whatever it takes. There's always counselling, it's confidential, Jack, you know that, between you and them. I don't need to know about it, except that you're going." She pressed her lips together, an expression I recognised. She knew I wouldn't accept; like most cops, I wasn't keen on counselling. But she had to offer it.

"Okay, okay. But not yet. Let me put the scumbag away first. I have to do this." I stared at her. "My Maddy is the same age as Jessica."

"I know," she sighed and dropped her head momentarily. "Okay, Jack. Go do what you got to do. But remember, after another murder's announced, they'll all be watching us. No more public outbursts, okay? No moments like you had with Richards."

"Yeah," I muttered and rushed away from Hicks and Holmberg towards the underground car park. Unlocking the car, I started it up, and settled in for the drive. Thankfully traffic wasn't too bad, and I mulled things over on the way.

The scumbag had planned this, and most likely abducted and abused before. So far, I had little to go on other than that we'd discussed taking DNA from Marlin Jones. So, the question remained; how had a weasel that abducted, sexually abused and then murdered little children evaded capture so far? Sweat formed at my temples, and I gripped the steering wheel tightly.

Eventually, following both Harry's directions and the map located on my phone, I pulled into the Sherbrooke Picnic Ground car park and parked at an incline. The usual inky darkness had been alleviated by a temporary spotlight. There were three other cars parked, most likely the detective and a couple of forensic investigators.

I locked the door, and opened the boot, where I found a heavy-duty torch, a pair of gloves, and my work boots. I sat on the edge of the car, changed into the boots, threw my dress shoes in, and stuffed the gloves into a pants pocket. I turned on the torch and shut the boot.

Other than the sounds of lyrebirds, the forest sat eerily silent, not even the sound of passing traffic. I aimed my torch at the edges of the cark park and swung it around looking for a sign.

I found one that said, *Sherbrooke Falls walk: 1.8km* and knew from my map that the creek should be about a kilometer in. With a sigh, I headed off. I used the torch to guide me along a path, really only a narrow section worn down by other walkers. I lifted my knees up high through the wet grass and did my best to push down the surging heat in my chest and the burning in my throat. I wasn't sure if the cause of the burning was the urge for another drink, or the thoughts of what Jessica Holmes went through before she died.

Instead, I took another deep breath and focussed on the impenetrable darkness, and the path in front of me, in a bid to push the thoughts away. It didn't stop the ache in my throat though. After walking for what was probably five minutes but felt like fifty, I saw a spotlight in the distance.

The murder scene.

As I got closer, I saw the tape set up, and the spotlight increased in size. I eventually could make out that it appeared to be on the incline of the bank on the other side of the creek to my left. The noise of lightly rushing water in the creek grew louder.

A figure in a forensic suit took photographs on the bank of the water, another dressed similarly bent over on the other side of the creek.

About three metres behind the doubled-over forensic tech, stood a woman with dark brown hair in what looked like office clothes. Her head hung low, hiding her face.

As the forensic tech stood and walked towards the woman, I made out his face. Jarrod Milne; we'd worked together on another incident, a murdered mother found in a car boot, a horrific case that was solved eight months later. I shivered and stopped a couple of metres from them both. They turned their heads in my direction.

I pulled my badge out of the inside pocket, flipped it open and stopped moving. The female detective was now about ten metres away.

The grass rustled beside her, and she took a small step towards me with her hand out slightly, offering a handshake. I walked slowly towards her and took her hand. "Detective Sergeant Rae Swanson, Maroondah," she said.

"Jack Fletcher," I said, in a voice rough even to my own ears. I walked closer, . "We spoke, in fact... a little while ago, about the murdered girl, Jessica," I added as we shook hands. I needed to say it to jog her recall. She simply nodded and smiled.

"Jarrod," I said then, nodding in his direction.

"Jack," Jarrod said, holding a camera in his right hand.

"Did you forget to call me back?" I said to DS Rae Swanson, not letting a simple smile answer why she hadn't done what she promised.

Detective Sergeant Rae Swanson looked to be in her late thirties, reasonably tall and brown pools of eyes that saw all. Except, how angry I was inside, the heat rising up the back of my neck.

"No." She swallowed hard, and her face looked like it had collapsed in on itself, flushed and possibly suppressing a whole lot of shit going on below the surface. I felt sorry for the woman now; this was a struggle I recognised.

"Louisa Fein," Rae said, staring at the creek, with fixed unseeing eyes. "Missing for three weeks. Her parents wouldn't give up hope, and I don't blame them. We all hoped she was abducted not murdered. The government pathologist will have to confirm it, but it's her, I'm sure of it."

"This looks like the case I called you about, Jessica Holmes. Remember—Jessica went missing six days ago. It would have been helpful to speak back then. But now we have to deal with it all over again."

"I'm sorry," she said. "Tell me about Jessica? I really am interested. It was just—"

I cut her off. I wasn't interested in hearing the *why*; we had to move forward for the sake of the girls' families and the safety of all the kids in the area. I told her about Jessica.

"She was found on the opposite side of this forest, in a different clearing. She was seven, and her parents called her in as a missing person four days before she turned up dead. Any idea of Louisa's cause of death?" I said.

Rae shoved her hands into the pocket of her grey jacket and looked down before lifting her head. Jarrod answered this time.

"Stabbed, through the chest, Nicki, one of the forensics techs, says she was probably sexually assaulted, but we won't know for sure until the autopsy's finished. Judging by the body, I'd say she's been here only a day or two, and possibly kept somewhere else before death at a guess."

"Thanks, Jarrod," I said.

Swanson didn't speak.

"Right, well, I better get back to it, then get her ready for transport," Jarrod said. He walked slowly back towards the creek.

"How did she disappear?" I said.

Swanson cleared her throat. "Playing at the local park; she was flying a kite with her older sister, and at some point ran off. When her sister went looking for her, Louisa was gone." Swanson's voice quieted at the end of the sentence. I wondered if this job ate at her like Jessica Holmes' case did with me? I wanted to talk to Swanson, ask if her case gnawed away at her like that, but couldn't get the words out past my sore, strangled throat.

"Which park did she disappear from?" I said.

"Fontane Park in Knoxfield," said Rae. Knoxfield was about a twenty minute drive from Sherbrooke forest, and ten minutes from Jessica's home in Croydon. The wind whipped Rae's hair back off her face, and I saw the angles and hollows. I wondered if she'd sleep tonight after today's visit to the crime scene of another murdered child.

"Jessica Holmes disappeared from a park in Croydon, directly opposite her home," I said, watching Rae carefully. In the harsh reflection from the spotlights, her face looked hollowed out, with deep rivets and valleys holding lines of shadows, more so than someone in her late thirties at a guess.

She acknowledged my statement with a nod then turned to face me. "So, you think our jobs are all related? The two other girls, Taylor and Bianca?" she said, eyes widening.

"Yes. Jessica and Louisa, especially. They're all part of Project Beacon now. The park the bodies were found in, and their ages are similar. Suspects don't abuse, abduct and murder children on a whim. Jessica disappeared four days before her body was dumped in this national park. But it sounds like, if it's the same scumbag, he took and maybe killed Jessica first, then Louisa," I said, scuffing my boot on the dried leaves.

"Yeah, these murders are rough," she said, not elaborating further. Rae Swanson's hands were still shoved in her pockets.

"Jessica was sexually assaulted, but I wonder if he took Louisa first; you say she went missing weeks ago. I wonder if he killed her first, but she died quickly, so to satisfy his sick twisted mind, he drew Jessica's killing out and tortured her before he finally raped and killed her."

"It's....Louisa's body. Her dark hair... and she looked just like an angel. The suspect left her body naked, with her hair still in a ribbon, you know? Her hands were crossed and placed over her chest, covering an open, bloodied stab wound..." Her voice faltered like any officer's voice shouldn't, but sometimes did. Swanson paused. "I can't forget, it's imprinted in my mind. I mean, how? How can anyone—"

She looked away at the creek, probably so I didn't see how close she was to cracking up. I carried on as if I hadn't noticed; she wouldn't be grateful for sympathy.

"Yeah, child murders do that, Rae. We probably won't forget. Imagine how the families are doing. Yeah, try to focus on the families; that's what I do," I said. It sounded lame. Swanson didn't know about my own tortured state of mind, the dreams, the tears, the fall-outs. I was being the big man. And it was working... except inside myself.

Swanson didn't reply.

"This is a serial killer, I'm sure of it. I had a suspect but can't pin him down yet. Can you let me know what you come up with?"

"Yeah," she said quietly. "I'll wait for the autopsy and let you know. I want to find the killer too, Jack, badly."

"Okay. We're agreed on that," I said, softly. "Night, Rae." I flicked on my torch and turned away to walk back into the forest towards the car park.

CHAPTER ELEVEN

SHARDS OF LIGHT PIERCED the curtains and stung my gluey eyes. It was Autumn, but my clothes clung to me, and sweat ran through my hair. My left arm had gone to sleep, hung over the side of the chair, grazing the wooden floor. I shifted in my seat, grimacing. My head pounded.

Another fucking hangover. I checked my watch. 5:10 a.m. I wondered if the images during sleep, of Jessica running away from an orange van had woken me, or the light.

It was a toss-up between another bottle of whiskey, the job, or broken sleep as to the cause of the shitty situation. Might as well go to work, than sit stewing in my own juice.

I showered, changed and threw back a mug of steaming black coffee. I arrived at my desk around 7 a.m. Daylight had only just broken about forty minutes earlier.

I threw my keys on the desk, booted up the computer and wandered towards the kitchen to make coffee. As I slotted a filter in the coffee machine, the sound of a flushing toilet and a rushing tap filtered out from the men's bathroom.

I heard a light sound of padding on carpet, then Garrett appeared in the kitchen.

"Hey, Jack, couldn't sleep either, huh?" he said. He didn't seem worried about his unshaven face and tousled hair, but then we'd known each other for years and been through some shit together. Besides, appearances were the least of our worries with the current hours we were working.

"Something like that," I said to my mug of coffee, strong and black.

"Still on the Holmes murder? Kids' cases are rough." Garrett moved to stand beside me. I watched as he emptied coffee grinds from the scoop into the filter and shut the lid of the machine. Light streamed in through the frosted glass window.

"Yeah." I turned, folded my arms and leaned against the kitchen bench. Garrett ran one hand through his tousled hair and blew out a breath.

"Sometimes, I wonder why I'm still in this job." Garrett turned towards the kitchen door, with his back to me. He paused and turned halfway back. "Pam keeps telling me to get help, or resign, but I told her my job is to find the bad guys, not moan about it. She doesn't get it."

I opened my mouth then closed it, thinking better of a sudden spontaneous rush of confession. Obviously, my lack of sleep and abundance of alcohol had contributed to my tendency to hit the accelerator before engaging the clutch. I wanted to tell Ed Garrett about the nightmares, about the drinking, the trouble with Abbie, but decided against it. It wouldn't help either of us.

We'd worked together for years, and I trusted him, but some things, they couldn't be said out loud, they were just too private. Garrett was right, the cases left a mark on us, but the victims' families had it worse. Until I'd done my job and found the scumbag raping and killing children, there was no time for the luxury of talking about my feelings, about every damn brain fart to some counsellor more interested in taking notes than anything else.

I pushed myself forward and away from the bench and took another step toward Garrett. We were only two feet away from each other. His breath smelled of stale tobacco and too-strong coffee. "I feel like that sometimes too, mate. But some-one's got to find these bastards, if only for the family's sake. Sometimes, I wonder if the job's worth it, but somehow, I keep going. Worst thing we could do is nothing."

Garrett mumbled something under his breath, and I followed as he headed through the kitchen door back towards the arrangement of four laminated grey desks. Garrett landed heavily on his desk chair, positioned opposite mine.

I sat in my blue office swivel chair and pulled it towards the desk. I glared at the paperwork on my right, nestled up beside a book end. I fucking hated paperwork but resisting never helped.

I grabbed the sheaf of papers, ready to go over them again, fresh, and in a new moment in time. Then I decided to put off the paperwork for a bit longer by opening my email program, where there were hopefully more leads from the Crimestoppers program.

"What's the plan today?" said Ed. I spun around. He had his back to me now, clicking on the computer mouse.

I spun back to my tiny screen. "Back to basics. Whenever I got nothing, back to the joy of administration. How about you?"

"Same deal," Garrett said. "Going through the Crimestopper tips. Always an education."

I scrolled through my inbox. Ninety-eight unread emails. Where the hell did these things come from? I didn't even like to eat spam, let alone read it. I sighed, I'd left it too long between checking them. I scrolled down to the oldest ones and began opening them. A couple of callers had tips about suspicious people walking past their houses, but they ultimately gave little. One lunatic said Jessica Holmes was still alive, he'd seen her walking into school when he walked his dog that morning. I deleted the email. That and the usual memos and internal marketing emails.

Thirteen ignored, one deleted. Who the hell invented email anyway? A torturer?

The crazies and the desperate usually surfaced around Crimestoppers, especially if there'd been a plea in the media for information, but I needed to go through all of them. All I needed was one, one solid lead.

Behind me, Garrett stared at a sheaf of papers, bringing them close to his face. Probably had a night on the piss too.

I scrolled up to more recent Crimestopper emails. Scanning the email subject titles, two words stood out. 'CCTV footage.' I held my breath and sat stiffly, afraid to move. I felt frozen there. CCTV...

The email said a bank manager from a local bank about two kilometres away, at Bank East, had some information. After hearing the story in the news, security guards had found some footage that looked suspicious. A young blonde child, a girl, had been seen running directly outside the bank on the day Jessica Holmes went missing.

I licked my cracked lips and flicked a glance at the photo of Abbie and the girls on my desk. Happier times. Back then, I'd actually had time for them and almost had my shit together.

"Holy shit," I whispered.

"What?" Garrett said, twisting in his seat towards me. That guy could hear a fart in a space suit.

I stood up abruptly and my office chair spun towards the middle of the cordoned-off area that housed four desks. I grabbed my jacket from the back of the seat, scooped up my keys and wallet and—despite the headache and sweats from the night before— managed an excuse of a smile. "Crimestoppers lead,"

"Oh yeah?"

I'd begun walking away from Garrett towards the car park, but he called out as he strode down the corridor

"What's the go, mate?"

"Bank manager, saw Jessica running out the front of the bank! Later, Ed."

I shoved the back door open and hit a jog to get to the car. Bank East in Croydon would be a reasonable drive if I took the freeway, especially at this time of day. I got in, started her up and reversed as fast as humanly possible, spun the steering wheel to the right and headed out the driveway, waiting to get out onto Spencer Street. I turned on the radio and took a couple of deep breaths to slow down my heart rate, but couldn't shake the feeling that this was it, the lead that would get me somewhere. A turning point.

As I waited at a set of lights before I hit the freeway, I thought about the CCTV footage. I hoped that not only was it Jessica Holmes running in front of the bank, but that maybe the killer had been stupid enough to pass by too, or at least show his registration plate. After ten minutes of throwing up possible scenarios in my mind, I began to relax a little, courtesy of the open freeway and focussing on one task, driving.

My phone rang. I hit the button on the steering wheel to answer the call safely, on Bluetooth.

Caller ID read, "Gary Holmberg."

"Yeah?"

"Where you at? Another lead?"

"Yeah."

"Where to?"

"Bank East, Croydon,"

"Quite a drive,"

"Nearly there."

"What's going on?"

"Since when did you give a shit, Gary?"

"Since now. Must be worth something or you wouldn't be so fucking secretive about it. This isn't the Wild West, Jack"

"It's Croydon, the Wild East."

"Since when were you a lone operator?"

"Since now."

Gary hung up.

I wasn't in the mood for twenty questions. I just wanted to drive. I listened to the Arctic Monkeys asking, 'Do I want to know?"

I did. Badly. I took the Ferntree Gully Road exit, and five songs later, pulled up at a largely vacated shopping centre car park called Mountain Gate.

I got out and looked around. Reasonable-sized shopping centre on the corner of Burwood Highway and Ferntree Gully

Road. I locked the car and walked the few steps to the bank's front entrance. Inside was all quiet heat, navy blue carpet and middle-class suburban activity, tellers behind secure screens, and three customers queued waiting to be served, standing obediently next to a red rope hung between metal stands.

I walked towards the nearest staff member, seated at a desk. Marg wore a name badge, and a navy uniform. Reaching for the inside left pocket of my camel-coloured jacket, I flashed my ID at Marg, along with my best attempt at a smile.

"Detective Sergeant Jack Fletcher. The Manager, Brett Jones contacted Crimestoppers. He has some CCTV footage of interest to us in a murder case. I'd like to see the footage please."

Marg looked up at me with eyes wide, took her right hand off the mouse, and stood up slowly. She was short and round, maybe five foot three.

"I'll just see if I can find Mr. Jones," she said quietly and moved off to the back of the office. I watched her walk to a wooden door where she entered a security code and disappeared. I shoved my hands in the pockets of my jeans, stared at the blue carpet then looked up to see faces turned in my direction. Most of them looked away, embarrassed, other than one old lady who stared back for a moment, then turned again to the teller.

Within a few seconds, the heavy door at the back clicked open again and a balding man emerged. He was short, plump, and wore a blue suit that matched the carpet. The remains of his hairline were black. He walked towards me and, at about the two-foot mark, extended his right hand outwards.

"Brett Jones, Manager." His handshake was firm. As he let go, he sighed, and handed a business card over. "Nasty business, happy to help. Please come through."

"Thank you." I followed Brett through the heavy door, feeling the stares of staff and customers burning through the back of my head.

I followed him through the doorway and veered to the left a few paces, walking down a corridor for a few metres. The carpet changed colour from blue to a nondescript beige. A grey door sat at the end of the corridor. Brett gestured to it with his left hand and pushed it open.

"My office. I had security bring the footage in here; thought it might be more private. We won't be disturbed."

"I'm not sure how long I'll be. I'll take a look now, then take a copy with me if possible," Jack said.

"Of course," Brett said, frowning. He didn't sit. "I'm sorry about the delay in getting the information to Crimestoppers, but I was at meetings, busy. You know how it is." He looked embarrassed, his expression pained. "Security only brought the footage to my attention a few days ago. I called it in as soon as I could." He shoved his hands in his pockets and shifted his weight from one foot to the other.

"It's okay," I said. While it was infuriating, making him wrong wouldn't help either of us, and I wanted to see what was on the tape. It was what mattered now.

"The footage may well help us. We appreciate all tips," I said. And as I said it, I knew I was spinning the police PR line. Truth was, we didn't appreciate all tips, some came from crackpots, some a complete waste of time, but I knew better than to upset the applecart and discourage callers to the Crimestoppers line. Even if it had been a lifetime ago, I'd made a promise to serve and protect.

If the Crimestoppers line dried up after word spread that police didn't want the tips, then a cop's job got a hell of a lot more difficult.

Brett finally sat down, leaned over his computer and clicked on the mouse. "I'll set up the footage," he said. "Then I'll leave you to it."

"Thanks." My stomach churned, and my throat swelled. This might be the lead I desperately needed, but then again it might not. The number of times I'd had a 'feeling' and it had let me down were too many to count. While I'd tried not get my hopes up with this one, it hadn't fully worked. I ached to see the footage but felt compelled to give the appearance of being cool, calm and in control. I couldn't give any indication of this desperation, not a hint, not a smell of it.

The security footage appeared on the screen, paused. Brett stood up and moved sideways away from the desk, across from me as I leaned in the far corner to let Brett set everything up. Then Brett walked over and stood at the door, one hand on the doorway.

"I'll come back in ten minutes, okay? How does that sound?"

"Perfect." My pulse hammered in my throat, and blood rushed in my ears. Brett closed the door behind me. The first thing I noticed was the time on the bottom right of the screen, around ten minutes to eleven. Jessica Holmes and her sister were at the park at roughly ten in the morning and her sister Gemma had got home around twelve noon. I pushed a button to speed up the footage to around one a half times normal speed. I waited. And waited some more.

Then there she was.

I shifted forward in the seat and leaned over to get a closer look. The hair, the clothes; it was her. I knew Jessica almost like one of my own daughters. My arms prickled up and I swallowed, hard.

She was wearing the clothes her father had described on the day she went missing. Jessica had her back to the camera, and the wind blew her long blonde hair. An orange van pulled up from the right and stopped in front of the camera. Jessica opened the back door, and got in. I couldn't see the driver.

My pulse went into overdrive, and I rewound the footage. I replayed it, homing in this time on the driver's side, to identify the driver. Nope, that part of the vehicle was shadowed; the driver couldn't be identified.

Fuck it.

I jiggled my leg underneath the desk. I replayed the footage again, hoping for a registration plate.

Nothing.

Shit.

I paused the footage, stood up quickly and walked out of the room, searching for the bank manager. I needed a copy of that footage.

Now.

The last known sighting of Jessica Holmes on CCTV was my best lead so far.

I wouldn't give up on her.

CHAPTER TWELVE

TECHNICALLY, THE NEXT day was glorious. The perfect temperature, not too warm, not too cold, sunny without a hint of wind.

But there was no perfect day for the funeral of a little girl, seven-year-old Jessica Mae Holmes. I looked down at the front cover of the service booklet for the funeral and rubbed my left thumb over her picture. Holmberg, Garrett and I waited at the bottom of the pale concrete steps outside the Chalmers Rose funeral home in Upper Ferntree Gully, not wanting to intrude too much.

On the way there we hadn't bothered talking about being anonymous; cops stood out like dogs' balls, with or without a uniform. Besides, as usual, the media were still all over this one. They'd arrived earlier than us, taking pictures from the other side of the street. Holmberg, Garret and I left them to Tracey from the media unit, who'd already arrived. She was talking to them. Thankfully, the cameras and stares had stopped. We wanted to pay our respects not deal with journalists.

We'd arrived there, with only a few mourners congregated in the area roughly fifteen minutes earlier. We were all waiting for the service to start, awkward and unsure, forming clusters at the bottom of the steps, on the outdoor porch, and inside the main foyer.

We'd taken a walk around when we arrived, to get a feel for things, and register the faces of attendees.

I'd memorised as many faces as possible. We took a step up to the glass entry doors, where sweet music piped through the speakers in the plushly-carpeted foyer, and the light scent of flowers clung to the furnishings. Just inside the foyer, Will Holmes stood on the left surrounded by what could only be close family. One dark-haired man with a moustache draped an arm around Will's right shoulder, while an older lady with grey hair in a bun supported him on the right.

We took a couple of steps in their direction, our steps silent on the carpet. Holmberg stopped about a meter from the trio. "I'm so sorry. My condolences," he said quietly.

Will had shaved and changed into a suit, but it didn't disguise his grief. Head bowed, his shoulders curled in on himself, he sniffed as he lifted his head. Pale and drawn, he looked as though the life had been sucked out of him. Eyes reddened, he looked directly at me and spoke with lips quivering, struggling to speak.

"Find them. Find the bastard, for me, for my girl." His voice was subdued and gravelly. His face collapsed in on itself and his mouth contorted as he sobbed. The man and the woman made soothing, hushing noises and the woman pushed a handkerchief into Will's hand. She glared at us as they ushered him away.

"I'll find him," I mumbled but Will Holmes didn't hear me, lost in a world of grief and despair.

I turned and walked back outside, followed by Garrett and Holmberg. We walked down the steps, and stood on the outskirts of the groups of mourners.

I rubbed my forehead, wondering how the hell I would keep my whispered promise to Will Holmes?

"Oh, God," this time Garrett mumbled, barely heard.

Holmberg straightened up, his attention caught by a lone man walking along the street, past the media, at the edge of the downward-sloping driveway. The man stopped walking and stared back at us briefly before increasing his stride. "Is that the suspect? Marlin Jones?" Holmberg kept his voice low, frowning hard.

"Huh?" I said, snapping my head up. "Jones? You're fucking kidding me."

With a tilt of his head, Garrett pointed him out.

"Marlin Jones, you piece of shit," I growled. In a split second I took off at a run towards him, oblivious to the media and the crowd. I'm sure all heads turned in my direction, but at that point I couldn't care less; all I cared about was bringing Jones down. Judging by the panting and curses behind me, Gary Holmberg took off as well as Ed Garrett.

Marlin Jones sprinted along the street and veered off into a no-through road, where thankfully there was little to no traffic. My chest hurt like hell and so did my arms and legs, but I ran like I hadn't run in a long time. Jones swung into a small park with me sprinting after him about ten metres behind. I needed to close in on him. Ignoring the pain, I pushed ahead, and gained a couple of metres. I thought my chest would burst and my head explode.

A red-haired man pushed a toddler on the swings. If he swung out to the left and put his arm out, he could grab Jones who was almost there.

"Police! Stop that man!" I yelled with the last of my air. I sprinted forward with every bit of energy left. Every desperate wish, every alcohol-soaked nightmare propelled me forward.

Grab him. Now.

The red-haired man moved sideways from the swing towards Marlin, grabbing at his jumper and spinning him backwards. Marlin screamed. The toddler began to cry. The red-haired man backed away.

"Get off me you fucking bastards!" he roared, screaming more obscenities and swinging wildly in an attempt to get away and land punches on one of us.

In a second, I caught up and I grabbed both Marlin's arm's, pulling him to the ground. I wrenched them fiercely behind his back and pushed Marlin to the earth, grinding my right knee into his back. I gasped for breath.

"That's what they all say. Shut it, there's kids here." I pulled harder on his hands. "Shut it, or I'll hurt you, I swear." Marlin's screams died down to whimpers.

Ed dangled a set of cuffs in front of me just within reach. I snatched them and swung them into my hand, lowering myself to secure Marlin's hands at the front of my knees, which were still in his back. He let out a high-pitched squeal, much to my satisfaction.

Holmberg stood at Marlin's head, heaving to catch his breath as I snapped the cuffs onto Marlin's wrists. We got him.

I looked at Garrett who moved over to stand on the other side of Marlin, face squashed into the dirt. I looked to the red-haired man who now held the young boy and was speaking soothingly to him.

"Thanks," I said.

"I'll take your details." Garrett took a step towards the man, notebook ready.

"Let's take him back to the station." My voice caught between breaths, wavered. Garrett and I yanked Jones up to a standing position. He tried bending his knees.

"Don't bother, there's three of us,"

Jones straightened up slightly. "Maybe we need to push him against the fence, so he gets the idea." Garrett didn't bother holding back his anger.

Jones stood up straight.

Garrett and I grabbed an elbow on each side of Marlin and pushed him back down the path to the street, and to their parked vehicle.

"I didn't do anything! This is illegal!" yelled Marlin. None of us was buying what he was selling.

"Why did you run?" snarled Garrett, who I figured now had Red Hair's details. The man had his back to us, walking quickly down the path.

Marlin didn't answer as we bundled him into the car, got in and headed back to the station.

BACK IN THE CITY AT Crime Command, Marlin was brought through the sliding doors, and shoved into a tiny interview room until we worked out how we'd play it and which charges to throw at him. At that point, obstructing an investigation and some type of stalking charge looked good.

"Let me take him, Ed." I leaned against the wall in the corridor outside the interview room. Ed's shirt was rumpled, hair in disarray. I hadn't bothered worrying about how I looked, other than the comb my hair received when I'd run my fingers through it in the car. Lucky if I had any black hair left after the drive with Jones in the back. Surprisingly, only a few had gone grey. Ferntree Gully to the city had been a hell of screaming and lashing out. Thankfully, the plexiglass barrier and the radio had blocked the bastard out.

Holmberg appeared, and put his hands on his hips. "Mate, not a good idea. You're likely to deck him; you know what the brass will do. Better we both interview him."

I dug my hands deeper into the pocket of my pants. "It'll be fine, Gary. I want this guy bad, but I'll keep it cool, okay?"

Holmberg didn't answer.

"Half an hour, okay? Gimme half an hour with him. If I'm not out in that time, you can come in and umpire."

Gary Holmberg dropped his chin and walked away down the corridor, towards his desk.

He didn't look back. Considering the lack of conversation, Garrett had given up at this point. He blew out a breath, shook his head and followed Holmberg.

I sighed and looked around. Just another day in paradise, cops and office workers staring at screens and paperwork. I opened the interview door. Marlin sat on the other side of a small table that was nailed to the floor. He rested his elbows on it, pointing the steeple of his fingers at the top of his nose.

He lifted his head as I sat down. There were no windows in the room at all.

"This will go a whole lot easier if you spit it all out,"

Marlin sneered. "You sound like a TV show."

"You already lied to us more than once. You didn't tell me about your history of sex offences against children, and you said you weren't at the park the day Jessica disappeared. We know you were."

Marlin barely batted an eyelid. "But I didn't kill her."

"Witnesses placed you at a park, the kids' playground, they saw you talking to Jessica, saw your truck at the playground, you have a background. And now, today, you show up at the funeral." I breathed slowly. *Calm and professional, Jack, play it cool, stay calm and do your job.* My fists were clenched under the table, resting on my knees. I slowly released my fingers from their death-like grip.

Marlin leaned forward. "I wanted to pay my respects, that's all, she seemed like a nice girl."

Blood sped through my veins, electrical current sparking. I brought my hands up to the desk and linked my fingers together. "So, you admit you talked to her?"

"Yeah, I talked to her, but that's all. Last time I saw her she ran back to play so I went home."

"You don't see anything weird about a registered sex offender hanging out a park where children play? Then turning up at the funeral of a little girl that was murdered at the same park?"

The legs of the chair scraped as Marlin shifted his chair on the linoleum floor. "I already said, that was a long time ago. I did my time. I didn't kill her."

"Did you abduct her? Then kill her? Show up to the funeral to view your handiwork?" I'd tried so hard to stay cool but it burst out like a firecracker. I'd told myself I wouldn't lose my temper, but the more I tried to convince myself, the worse it got. My heartbeat bashed against my ribcage, and my face burned.

"No, I didn't take her, my record is history now, I did my time. I told you, I didn't kill her." Marlin's voice changed in pitch, higher, almost a squeal. The worm protested too much. Time to try a different angle.

"If it's all just a misunderstanding, you won't mind taking a DNA test. A swab of your saliva will be enough." I straightened up in my chair, and eyed Jones off.

Marlin dropped his gaze to the table, then looked back up. "Am I under arrest? Because if not, I'd like to go home now. I've had better days."

Marlin's collar was only inches from my hands, palms down on the table now. It would take a split second to yank his collar, lift him up off the floor and fling his puny spine against the wall.

I kept my voice quiet, controlling my rage, deep and low. "Yes. You'll be charged with impeding an investigation and further changes are pending. An officer will be in shortly to begin that process. As far as the rape and murder of Jessica Holmes, we need to eliminate you as a suspect. A DNA test will do that."

Marlin stood up. "So, you chased me for what? Because I pissed you off? Stood on your turf? As for murder, you're guessing. Sounds more like harassment to me." Marlin flung his hands up in the air.

I paused. I needed a moment to compose myself, to wait for the seething pressure in my head to subside. My hands were back under the table, resuming the clenched fist position, but now my nails bit into my palms so hard my palms stung, and something dripped. Possibly blood. "Sit down." I spoke through clenched teeth. "I'll get the officer to see you and formally charge you as soon as possible. And I'll get the DNA kit."

I stood up slowly, rising to all six foot two of my frame, glaring at Marlin. Marlin might be a dirt bag, but he still had some sense left. He sat back down.

I took a couple of steps towards the black locked cupboard on the back wall of the interview room, unlocked it and reached for a plastic bag. I found it, removed it from the cupboard, locked up again and walked back to the table. I didn't sit. I removed a swab from the plastic bag and unscrewed the lid of the pathology container.

"Open your mouth as wide as you can." I had managed to park my emotions. Marlin leaned forward to comply. I stuck the swab into his mouth and swiped both sides. I put the swab back in the container, screwed on the lid and put it back in the plastic bag. I wrote "Marlin Jones," on the outer label, suppressing the desire to write "Filthy Scumbag."

Marlin sat back in the chair. "Can I go now?"

I pressed my lips together. "No."

Marlin didn't speak; he simply stood up and pulled at his cuffs, screaming about the injustice of it all. I sat at the table and waited for my blood to shift from simmering and back to normal, clenching my fists.

I wanted to lock the worm up for murder, but without evidence, I'd just have to eat it, the frustration, the constant fraying of my mind as I thought of little Jessica Holmes. I still kept her photograph with me, but it had moved from the pocket of my trousers to the inside of my jacket.

I got up and strode out, the door closing on Marlin's bullshit. I pushed out a breath and headed for my desk. Holmberg was still there, pecking at a keyboard.

I stopped and stood beside him.

"He'll be charged, but not with murder—yet."

Holmberg turned away from the screen and looked at me. "Yeah well, I don't like letting it go either, but without evidence..."

"Yeah, might follow up on the search warrant for Marlin's place. He agreed to a DNA test, but who knows how long that will take."

Thankfully, Holmberg didn't say out loud what I suspected. It would be days or weeks before test results came back. At least now though, my blood flowed at normal speed and my heart pumped along regularly rather than barrelling along at full force.

My desk phone rang, and I strode across to grab it "Jack Fletcher,"

"Jack, it's Rae Swanson. About the Louisa Fein case."

"Yeah, got any news for me?"

"I got the DNA results back. No match. Whoever killed Louisa isn't in our DNA register," Swanson sighed.

I knew without a doubt the scumbag that killed Jessica Holmes, also killed Louisa Fein. I offered up a silent prayer he wouldn't kill again.

CHAPTER THIRTEEN

THE NEXT MORNING, HUNCHED over my desk after the painkiller kicked in, I went through the bank CCTV footage again. I must have gone through it a hundred times, scanning, desperate for anything.

Still nothing more.

Garrett arrived and hung his jacket on the back of his chair but didn't sit down.

"You might be interested in this one, Jack," he said, an edge to his voice.

"In what?" I said, twisting around in my chair to look at him. He stood in front of his office chair, hands in his pockets, gazing at the carpet. Eventually, he looked back in my direction.

"We picked up a pervert up today, exposed himself to a young girl. David McElroy. A bystander called it in."

My gut twisted. "Where is he?"

"In the interview room. He'll be charged with indecent exposure; thought you might like to talk to him before he goes to lock-up, might have some information for Project Beacon."

"Thanks, Ed," I said. I rubbed my right palm over my face. "Any priors?"

"Yeah we picked him up last year for exposing himself in public. Got probation for a first offence. But, get this. He drives an orange van, like the one in the CCTV footage. I checked the registration details. It's him."

My stomach felt empty and my throat burned.

"Let me at him," I growled, standing up. I took a few strides towards the doorway which led towards the front where the interview room entrance lay, just off the main corridor.

Homicides were one thing, but rape and sexual assault on children another, and I didn't like the world we'd fallen into. I'd headed down into the murky world of child paedophilia and needed a cold shower and a stiff drink.

Garrett followed me and stopped a foot away. "Jack, the world of sickos can wear a man down. But leave it alone, hey? Talk only. Don't touch him." I turned to face him. Ed Garrett watched me closely, looking for some sign I was losing it. He looked as bad as I felt. But I figured if I could play it cool with Marlin Jones, I could keep calm with this pervert.

"I'll play it by the book, Ed," I said. "But thanks for the heads-up." I continued walking and paused before the interview door to take a deep breath and get myself into the detachment of yesterday. Before I headed to the room, I grabbed a can of drink from the fridge, and shoved it in my pocket.

I opened the door. David McElroy sat at a rickety interview desk the size of a small card table, seated on a plain black chair. The scumbag might appear regular enough to most people, although first impressions of his appearance struck me as weasellike.

He was rail-thin, with pasty skin and black short hair plastered to his head. He looked up briefly when I entered, revealing a worm of a moustache, then hung his head. He wore a grey hoodie and what looked like matching pants. I took two strides towards the table and sat down across from him. I pulled the can of drink from my pocket and placed it on the table. McElroy grabbed it, opened it, and began drinking.

"Mr. McElroy? I'm Detective Sergeant Fletcher. I'd like to talk to you about what happened today."

The pervert lifted his head and looked directly at me. "I don't know what came over me," he mumbled. "It was stupid." His voice had a whining tone, grating.

"Yes, well. I wanted to talk to you about that, and I hoped you'd help with my enquiries. Do you mind if I record our interview?"

"I guess it's okay."

So far, McElroy hadn't asked for a solicitor, so we were good to go. I set up the recorder and began first with the date, the location, and the name of the two people in the room.

"Mr. McElroy, I understand you're likely to be charged with indecent exposure, following an incident earlier today. However, I'd like your assistance with an incident that occurred four days ago in Croydon. Can you tell me where you were around 11 a.m. on the 12th March?"

"Um, I don't remember exactly. What day was that?"

"The 12th was a Tuesday," I said. A day I'd never forget. The day Jessica Holmes was abducted outside the bank. The day I'd told Will Holmes his girl wasn't ever coming back.

"Uh, I'm pretty sure I ran a few errands, some shopping, banking, that kinda thing." McElroy rubbed his chin, then stared at the wall behind me.

"So, you were at Bank East around that time on the 12th June?"

"I don't remember the exact time, but it's possible, yeah. I bank with them and was there on that day." He took a drink, paused and looked at me directly. "What is this about?"

David McElroy struck me as unusually cooperative. At the prospect of being arrested and charged, most offenders were definitely not so willing to answer direct questions. It was time to get to the point.

I dragged my chair closer to the table. "Your orange van was seen outside the bank, and a little girl Jessica, was bundled into the car. Jessica's body was found some time later." I let the statement hang in the air.

McElroy wasn't quite so quick to answer this time.

"I had nothing to do with that. I don't go around killing kids," he said quietly.

"Why, then, was there a car outside the bank, with the same appearance and registration as your car, and why did a child—who later turned up murdered—get into it?" I'd never seen the plates, but I wasn't about to tell McElroy that.

McElroy no longer met my gaze and cleared his throat. He paused for a while longer this time.

"I had nothing to do with that girl. I'm not a murderer," he said again. Although he was no longer staring at me, McElroy had progressed to now staring at his hands on the interview table, rather than staring at his feet.

"You admitted you were there at the bank at that time, on that date. It was your vehicle, and a murdered child got into it. Jessica Holmes."

"Anyone could have used the car."

"Yes, they could have, but you've already admitted you were outside the bank at that time and on that day. Why did you do it? Same reason you exposed yourself in public? For cheap thrills?"

McElroy lifted his head. His eyes appeared glassy black, blank and soulless without a trace of light. "I told you. I had nothing to do with that girl's disappearance, or her murder."

"You haven't explained how your orange van was outside the bank on the day she went missing, or why she was seen getting into your car. Where did you take her? How did you kill her?"

A muscle flickered in McElroy's cheek. "I told you, I had nothing to do with that. I didn't kill anyone. Anyone could have had the car on that day."

"Such as? Who did you loan the car to? As you said, you were at the bank that morning, running errands. Let's be honest here. If I parked my car somewhere, I'd definitely notice if someone else broke into it and took it for a spin. For one thing, I'd call that theft and I'd report it to the police. So, what's your story? Either you loaned it, or you were using it yourself."

I reached over for a pen and notepad, pausing the pen over the pad, and looked at McElroy expectantly. I had my guy. The burning hot blades in my gut and the swirling storm in my chest told me this was him. This pervert, this worm...here was the scumbag that had tortured and killed little Jessica Holmes, Louisa Fein, and possibly the two others, Taylor Wentworth and Bianca Baker.

I decided to try a different tactic.

"This guilt, this bad feeling you may have inside, there is a way to get rid of it. And you know what that is, don't you?"

Stony silence. Again, McElroy met my gaze then looked down at his lap.

"I understand. I've been there. If you tell the truth, and tell me what happened, and get it out, you'll feel better."

After a couple of seconds, McElroy lifted his head and looked directly at me. "I'll talk to you, if you turn off the recording."

"I can't do that," I said.

"You want the truth, I'll give you the truth but no recording," he said, his voice edgy.

I hit the button and turned off the recording. I did my best to suppress the surge of anticipation. Finally, here and now, I'd get a confession and put this bastard away for a long, long time.

"I didn't abduct the girl you're talking about or kill anyone." McElroy paused, and he smiled slyly. "But I'm sure she was a sweet little girl, sweet and delicious,"

An inferno blew up, raging upward from my gut, blood racing through my chest and my neck. In a split second, I'd pushed back the chair—which scraped loudly on the old linoleum floor—and lunged forward, grabbing the worm by the collar and lifting him out of his seat. His eyes bulged, and he managed to blurt out, "What the..."

"You piece of shit, you fucking parasite! You killed those little girls, tortured them, raped them. I should..." I'd completely lost control, and in my rage, a tiny bud of saliva had landed on McElroy's collar.

The door burst open, and Garrett was by my side in a heartbeat, pulling me off David McElroy. I took a breath and dropped my hands.

Garrett didn't look at me at first, focussing on McElroy. "Please take a seat. An officer will be with you shortly," he said. McElroy was wide-eyed, straightening his shirt and beginning to hurl abuse at us both. Garrett had the presence of mind to take the electronic recording device and remove it from the room, grab a plastic bag to pick up the can, and then dragged me out, slamming the door shut.

"What the fuck happened to staying cool?" he hissed in the corridor outside the interview room. "Come on, let's get some coffee."

He shoved the recorder into his pocket, put the can inside a plastic bag, and strode off towards the kitchen, and I stumbled behind him, lost in thought. In the light-filled kitchen, I leaned back against the sink and closed my eyes, willing my heart rate to slow down and taking a couple of deep breaths. All I could think about was Jessica Holmes under the cold ground, beaten, raped, butchered—while her father wept.

Sure, I shouldn't have lost my cool, but something about this case had got under my skin, wormed its way in to gnaw at me, slowly dissolving the detective I thought I was. I hated that it had got personal. All I could think of was Will Holmes, his suffering, his grief.

He'd never get over this, and I wasn't sure if I'd ever forget it either.

Garrett focussed on getting some fresh coffee. He emptied the coffee pot and set up fresh coffee and filters, rather than dealing with me or looking at me. Maybe he needed to pause to get his bearings too. He flicked on the switch beneath the coffee pot and turned towards me, leaning one arm on the bench.

He shook his head. "Might be best to keep this between us for now; Hicks doesn't know about it, and McElroy might rant and rave, but without the recording, he's got nothing." He held the sealed bag containing the can out to me. "You might want to get this to the lab"

"Thanks," I mumbled and took the bag, staring at the floor for an answer that never came. As I lifted my head, I caught a presence leaning on the kitchen doorway to my right.

Selena Hicks.

Shit.

"I don't know about what?" she said and leaned further into the doorway.

Neither of us spoke. Eventually, Garrett opened his mouth to speak. I cut in ahead. "I interviewed a perp, McElroy. Indecent exposure charge. He's involved in the Holmes case, the little girl's murder."

"Project Beacon? The one with the media all over us? Tell me you didn't lose it again, Jack," she said, her voice quiet. One thing I'd learned was to keep my head down when boss lady got quiet. That usually meant I was in for a worse time than a show of direct anger from her.

Neither Garrett nor I replied.

"We'd better have a chat, my office. Now," she said and walked away. I trudged down the corridor to put the bag down, before heading for her office. I knew I'd get an ass-whooping. I hoped Hicks wouldn't take me off Project Beacon.

She entered her office and shut the door behind me.

"Sit," she said tersely.

I backed into the brown chair, inches away from her desk in her small office. I figured at that moment, it would be best if I said as little as possible.

"What the hell was that all about, Fletcher? Right now, you've got two options, spill your guts, or I find out later. I promise you, if I find out later that you didn't tell me everything, you're off Project Beacon." Her frown hardened, and she barely moved from her position, back ramrod straight and hands flat on her desk.

"A guy was pulled in and charged with indecent exposure, McElroy. He tried to grab a kid from the toilets in a shopping centre, got stopped by a member of the public. I have his vehicle on CCTV footage outside the bank. I can't see him inside the van, but I can see Jessica Holmes getting in the car."

"Go on."

"Garrett told me McElroy was in the interview room and being charged with indecent exposure. He checked the reg, and it matched McElroy's. So, I talked to McElroy. I might have grabbed him around the collar of his shirt."

"I see."

"He won't admit to any of it, the murder, the torture of that little girl. The rape. So, when he made a snide comment about her, I lost it..."

Hicks didn't speak.

"I might have said some things. Lifted him up by his collar. Ed stopped me."

I wasn't sure what I should be more worried about, Hicks getting angry, or her long drawn-out silence. Her hands were in the same position on her desk. She looked down at them, then back up at me.

"Were you recording this?"

"No, not that part. McElroy insisted I stop recording; I thought I'd get a confession out of him."

"Jack, level with me. You're not right. How are things at home?"

I didn't want to answer that, so I left it.

"It's not a bad thing to talk to someone. It will help. If you don't want to talk to a counsellor, talk to one of the other guys."

"Maybe I will," I said, knowing full well I wouldn't talk to anyone about what was going on at home. Some things were too private.

"I appreciate the honesty. But I'm going to have to ask you to go home."

"Again?"

"Jack, it's Saturday. Take a weekend off. Spend some time with your kids. Do the things that the rest of the damn world does; go out and live life."

"I think I'm finally getting somewhere."

"Maybe, but this is causing a problem with you. It's getting to you. I can see it, the whole team can. I'm not taking you off the case just yet, but I don't want you falling off the ledge, Jack. Take some time..."

I shook my head. I didn't like it, but I knew she was right. Truth be told, it could have been a whole lot worse. Hicks hadn't ranted, hadn't taken me off the case yet, but she was on to me. She might have a point. Maybe going home to see the kids, surprising them, and going out to the park, might be good.

I stood up. "Okay, boss, see you Monday."

Hicks looked up as I stood and walked away. I paused in front of her office door and turned to look at her.

"Go see your family, Jack."

CHAPTER FOURTEEN

I KNEW SOMETHING WAS wrong as soon as I pulled into the driveway at home. My head pounded, and my stomach churned. I put both hands on the steering wheel and closed my eyes.

Abbie's car wasn't there. I wasn't home that often, but when I did go home, Abbie was always there. She spent time either helping at the school one day a week, or shopping and running errands. Not that I would know anyway. Nowadays, I only really slept and ate there, and there hadn't been much of either of those two lately.

The darkness inside surprised me. The blinds were closed, no lights were on, and the shadows in the hallway, and the living room didn't exactly ease my worry.

Something was different somehow, the routine thrown out the window.

I put on hand on the stair railing and called up. "Anyone home? Abbie? Maddy? Molly?"

Nothing.

So, I called again. Still nothing.

Shit, I hoped nothing had happened to my wife, but then surely, she'd have called or sent me a text message if anything bad had happened. Right?

Wrong.

As soon as my feet hit the polished floors in the living room, I saw it in the semi darkness. A large envelope stood propped against the big screen TV, with my name scrawled in long, loopy writing across the front.

My wife Abbie's handwriting... I paced across the polished floorboards, rubbing at my forehead. My temperature must have jumped a couple of notches.

I opened the envelope and flicked open the page with my left finger. The words practically burned off the page.

'Jack, I almost wish we were back in the days where you'd yell at me. Now, all you do is ignore me. I wish you'd scream at me again. At least that way, I'd know you still cared. I know you're a detective, and you were when we married all those years ago, but you're different now. You've changed. Things have got to you. You keep on declining my calls. You're never here and show no interest in us. Am I that unimportant? Are your children? Do we mean so little to you? Do we need to become a rape or a murder job to get your damn attention? This is not the first time either. I love you and have always wanted to help you but despite all my efforts and my support of you and your career, what you've put me through in your quest to save the world isn't fair or deserved. You've had me in tears numerous times and barely noticed. All I want from you is an acknowledgment, a sorry, or some sense of responsibility for the promises we made to each other all those years ago.

I'm tired of being the dutiful spouse, to always be the under-standing one, to push my own needs aside all the time and just worry about yours. I can't continue to just brush each incident, each missed concert, missed dinner, missed milestone, under the carpet like it never happened. Don't you understand that every time you ignore us, or ignore me, I love you just a little bit less? Or don't you even care about that either?

I feel angry, hurt, infuriated, and devastated. Obviously to you, none of that matters. All you can see is that I don't understand, which is so off the mark, it's ridiculous. But then you don't know me anymore, and don't know your children, so how could you understand? And worse, I don't think you even try to. It's all about you, your life, and what you are doing at work. When did you last ask about me?

So, I've taken the kids to Nikki's to get some space, a bit of perspective.

I'll talk to you when I've calmed down and this has blown over a bit.

Abbie.'

My knees weakened, and I fell back onto the couch. I had no chance to get up and get a bucket. The dry heave came from nowhere. After I got my breath back, I pulled the phone out of my inside jacket pocket and dialled Abbie's number.

It rang and rang so long I wondered if she would let it go to voicemail. "Pick up the phone, pick it up Abbie, please," I whispered. "I'll change, I promise. Anything."

It rang endlessly, so it seemed. And now I thought about that line in her note, saying how I ignored her calls. So—this was what it felt like to get ignored? It was painful. Horrendous. And I rang and rang back, several times.

It rang for what seemed like forever... before the dialing finally stopped.

She didn't say hello immediately, but simply sat there on the phone waiting for me to speak. Eventually, she did.

"Jack?" I heard the quaver in her voice but didn't comment on it.

"I'm sorry. I'll do anything. Come home."

"Did you read the note?"

Another pause "Yes."

"And?"

"And you need to come home, this is crazy." My lungs constricted, making it hard to breathe. I extended the fingers on my right hand, staring at my nails, bitten down to the quick.

"You know what's crazy? Me being there as your invisible maid. I might as well be a single mother, Jack. We never talk, don't do anything together, you hardly sleep at home, staying up all night drinking, so what's the point anymore?"

"The point is, you're my wife." The muscles in my arms spasmed, so I rested my right elbow on the arm of the chair.

"In name only, Jack."

"What do you mean, *in name only*? Come home; the way to sort it out is together, not with you at your fucking sister's place."

"Like I said, I need some space, some time away."

"I need you here, not over there, so do the kids."

"How in the hell would you know what your kids need? You hardly ever see them."

"Please, can you maybe bring the kids back just for the weekend? Scratch that—I'll come and get them. The boss told me to take the weekend off."

"And why's that, I wonder? Has she seen what I've known for a while now? That you need help?"

"Abbie, what I need right now is you and the kids." I moved my left hand to my chest. My heart had slowed momentarily.

"No, what you need is to face the reality of the situation. There's no shame in getting help, Jack. It might be the start of something better, like it used to be."

"Just come home; we'll talk more when you get here."

"No. I meant what I said. I need some space. Once I can see things have changed, we'll talk again."

"Abb—"

She'd hung up. I didn't need to hold back the moan anymore. I screamed at an empty room. At the TV, the darkness, the empty scotch bottles standing in a line beside the armchair. I got up and kicked them.

Time stood still. No movement or sounds registered. A lone bird chirped. I tried to make sense of how we'd got to this point, with her giving up on our marriage and me alone in an empty house haunted by a little girl's life snuffed out, so far, an unsolvable case.

When we'd met, my promotion to sergeant had come through only weeks earlier, and I'd been accepted into detective school at the academy. We'd gone out to celebrate, me high on my own success, Abbie smiling shyly at my confidence. My prospects looked good, my career stretching up and out. I didn't want to be with anyone else, and Abbie felt the same, or so she said. Back then, we'd actually talked to each other, smiled, laughed, drunk, made love. We had fun back then. I didn't have a great deal of time back then either, but we'd gone out occasionally, dancing, drinking, kissing, and reveling in each other's company.

We only had eyes for each other.

Like most couples, the crumbling of our marriage had happened slowly; we'd got distracted, taken our foot off the accelerator. Or, it was taken off for us, first by young kids arriving on the scene, although admittedly Abbie had done most of the work there, and then it was work that gradually took the top spot in our lives. My wife wasn't earning, so I'd volunteered for as much overtime as I could get—the pressure to provide for my family bearing down on me. We just got stuck in the pattern, and the more work I did, the more I'd felt beholden to the job.

I'd been buoyed by hope, though; hope that if I worked hard and long enough, I'd put bad guys away no matter how difficult, or how long it took.

Then we'd refinanced the house, putting the kids into private schools, and I'd scored myself another promotion which kept up the mortgage payments. Abbie had seemed on board, and I'd never strayed, but then I'd never considered work would come between us rather than something terrible like an affair on either side.

We'd heard stories over the years of other couples separating, but it had usually been due to a third party, or so we'd thought. Maybe work had split up those other marriages too, but then none of our friends really talked about their relationships and it definitely wasn't something I'd ever talked about with Ed Garrett or any of the other guys at work.

So, we just kept on spinning the wheels of the daily grind, Abbie taking care of the kids and running the house. She did a great job and I preened, telling myself how smart I'd been in choosing her. We made sure the kids had everything they needed, me putting bad guys away, promotions every now and then, and working for what I thought was our future, and our kids' future.

As I dropped onto the floor, knees up, head in my hands, I knew now it had all been for nothing. No family, and four murdered children—and on a fast road to nowhere.

I knew the Holmes job had put me back, way back into the hole of drinking and pondering in a dark place, but I'd assumed Abbie would be where she always was, at home, guiding everything, my rock, the glue holding us all together.

But I guess even glue disintegrates over the passage of time.

I'd taken her for granted. I realised it too late, like most husbands, I supposed.

In a dazed stupor, I gazed at the wall where a family picture hung. The kids were much younger, toddlers, their faces innocent and their shining hair brushed with ribbons tied in bows. Abbie had worn make up and had her hair done for the picture, pressuring me relentlessly into doing it, saying we didn't have enough nice family portraits, if any at all. She wouldn't shut up about it, she'd worn me down.

So, I'd scrubbed up and put on my best gear. Hell, I'd even shaved and managed a smile for the click of the camera and the annoying woman telling me how to stand, to pose, to smile.

Now I'd been broken into a million pieces inside, each jagged edge spinning, digging in, cutting... until the pain became unbearable.

The spinning, almost unnoticeable earlier, sped up until I screamed and roared in protest, the roar coming from a place I didn't recognize and my voice that of an unknown person, disconnected, not mine at all.

I reared up from the chair and lunged at the picture, pushing it with one hand, knocking it off the picture hook. It bounced to the ground, landing with a heavy, sharp thud as it landed flat on the polished floorboards, the corner of the thick frame leaving a pointed dent in the wood.

I kicked the coffee table but it barely moved, so I spun around to the mantel piece, the shelf above the open fire we rarely used.

I let out a scream of rage, closed my eyes and pushed my hand quickly along the length of the mantel, shoving pictures, ornaments and other paraphernalia so they flew off the end. Some smashed onto the floor with a satisfying sound, while others catapulted across the room and hit the wall.

I clenched my fists and fell backwards, landing heavily onto the couch. My breath rasped heavily, and I gulped for air.

I couldn't remember the last time I'd done something like this, in fact, I didn't think it had ever happened. But the pressure had built up now, eventually blowing into a volcano of fury. Now it had erupted, I looked around at the room with fresh eyes.

Smashed porcelain littered the floor, and the head of an ornament lay a short distance from my right foot. I kicked away the staring eyes and watched as it smashed against the siding board of the back wall. The silence reminded me of the bleak fact that my family wasn't here, with no prospect of their return in the immediate future.

I reached across with my left hand, and opened the cupboard door, leading to my trusty stash of Jameson whiskey. My recent return to the days of old—drinking whiskey straight from the bottle—meant I'd been forced to actually pay the local bottle shop a visit and had stocked up. There were now three left, hiding in the cupboard beside the television.

I grabbed one of them and lifted it towards me. I grasped its neck with my right hand and twisted the cap until it opened with a click. I took a swig and the familiar heat making its way down into my chest soothed and greeted me like an old friend.

I thought about what the boss had said and toyed with the idea of talking to someone about the job, before quickly discarding it.

Sitting around talking about the case wouldn't bring relief; it would only make it more real, all too solid. I imagined the blank look of the counsellor, asking me personal questions about the case, my marriage, my relationships—and shuddered.

No, humans were imperfect and unpredictable; if nothing else, the point had been brought home in the light of the day's developments.

Better to rely on my old friend Mr. Jameson. I tightened my grip and took another swig. Unfortunately, in the light of my recent reacquaintance with the liquid amber, it took a good many more swigs than usual until the buzz kicked in and my shoulders relaxed. I rubbed my brow and got up to walk to the kitchen window.

I gazed outside at the backyard, where the swing set lay abandoned, and the toy bunny and scooter lay strewn nearby. Light pierced grey clouds, and flecks of rain decorated the window.

Something needed to break in the case soon, or the only thing left to break would be me. I needed the DNA sample taken from Jones to come back positive on Monday. If not, we were back to square one.

I wondered if I could take much more? If at that moment, someone had told me they could erase the last few days from my memory, I wouldn't hesitate. I'd tell them to lay it on me.

CHAPTER FIFTEEN

IT HAD TAKEN ALMOST a whole bottle of mouthwash first thing Monday morning, but I finally felt confident I'd evade boss lady's finely-tuned sense of smell. Without my wife or children home, I'd wallowed in my own thoughts and finished the last of the three Jameson bottles early Monday morning. Very early, in fact.

When I eventually reached the office, her radar peaked when I made it to my corner office cubicle, standing beside my computer to lean on the divider, her left elbow perched on top.

"How did the weekend treat you, Fletcher? Refreshed and ready for the next round?"

That was one way of putting it, I guess.

"I need to see the DNA results, I'm pinning my hopes on a warrant for DNA testing on McElroy." I'd evaded her question, didn't look at her either, instead just staring at my screen and clicking on an email I hoped was the result I desperately craved.

"Sounds good." Said Hicks.

"Okay."

"I've been thinking about this one, Jack. I think we need a meeting with the crew, great minds and all that."

I removed my hands from the keyboard. "Okay, when?"

"In the next few minutes. The boardroom's free, most of us are in the office, so no time like the present." She disappeared, leaving me to muse over her thoughts on the case. I wondered if she was considering calling in outside help.

I couldn't delay the inevitable for much longer, no matter how much I protested. In cases over child exploitation and sexual abuse, the SOCiT team would be notified. A Sexual Offences and Child Abuse Investigation team would want to be part of this one, and I had to admit, I could do with some help and added resources. I would have to cast aside my attachment to the case, no matter how reluctantly.

I trudged towards the kitchen for some coffee. Holmberg walked down the corridor towards me. "Looks like it's hotting up. I take it the boss filled you in on the meeting?"

"Yeah," I mumbled, adding sugar to the black coffee.

I followed him towards the boardroom. A few other officers I recognised, Ed Garrett, Andy Collen and Larry Weston were in there, already seated. Hicks chatted to Collen, and as Gary and I entered, she looked up.

"Gary, Jack. Shut the door behind you, will you?" Holmberg shot me a look and shut the door. We both took seats at the opposite end of the ten-seater table.

Pictures were pinned to the whiteboard, its arrows pointing in various directions.

"Okay, so Jack's been working intensively on the case, but I thought we'd share resources. The body of seven-year-old Jessica Holmes was found in Sherbrooke Forest a week ago. The body was staged, and she'd been tortured and sexually assaulted before death."

"Cause of death?" said Holmberg.

" Report came in over the weekend. Coroner's come back with a finding of asphyxiation," she said quietly. "So far, we've called in two people of interest." She turned and pointed to pictures of David McElroy and Marlin Jones. "DNA samples were taken from Jones, and we're ordering a test for McElroy, but unfortunately Jones didn't match the material found on either victim. I'll turn over to Jack now, and he can fill you in on developments."

Although it didn't really count as public speaking by most people's standards, I considered giving a briefing to colleagues to be up there with holding a press conference; I'd rather stick pins in my eyes. With several pairs of eyes on me, I pushed the chair back and stood up.

I cleared my throat. "Jessica Holmes went missing five days ago. She went to the local park with her sister and didn't come home. Gemma Holmes, her sister, saw a man in a red truck talking to Jessica before she went missing, asking her if she wanted to see his puppies." I suppressed the desire to roll my eyes.

"This man emerged to be Marlin Jones. He has a record dating back from ten years ago and was convicted of sex with a minor, which he failed to reveal when I visited him. He also lives on the same street as the Holmes family and was seen walking past the funeral. Collen and I arrested him on that day, and we have a search warrant which will be executed shortly. He agreed to a DNA test, but it has not matched the DNA found on Jessica's body." I hung my head and thrust my hands deep in my pockets.

"Other cases similar to this one?" I looked up at Gary Holmberg who'd asked the question. I felt fairly confident he knew about Louisa Fein, and that he just mentioned it so we all knew where we were at.

"Yeah, Louisa Fein, as well as two jobs from months ago, Taylor Wentworth and Bianca Baker, although those two girls were a few years older, and were suspected to be murdered by Dean Brown, convicted previously of rape and killed by a drug dealer recently. All murders other than Jessica Holmes had a slightly different MO, though. Louisa, Taylor and Bianca were stabbed, while Jessica was tortured and strangled. Both Louisa and Jessica were the same age, they were found in the same national park but not the same location, with both the bodies staged. Louisa went missing before Jessica did, but I figured whoever did this changed his methods to draw out the murder with Jessica. Maybe he figured Louisa died quickly, and I investigated possible links between the jobs. Maybe he wanted to draw out the last murder, make it last longer." A sour taste spread across my tongue, burning the back of my throat.

"And, any suspects on this Fein case?" Holmberg rubbed the bristles on his chin.

"Not as yet, I'm working closely with another detective on that one. We're holding David McElroy on a kidnapping charge due to the footage of his orange van and Jessica Holmes getting into it outside a local bank, but we have no other evidence to link either him or Marlin Jones to these two murders." A muscle flickered in my cheek. I wanted to charge him with both murders so badly I could taste the venom circulating in my system.

Hicks stood and moved to the whiteboard, so I sat down. "So, we need to finalise this one as soon as possible. As you can imagine, there's intense media interest in this, and the media unit's pressuring us, as is Regional Command. Jack's done a great job so far and is one hundred per cent committed to solving this one, but we may need additional resources."

She'd said it and voiced my concerns from earlier in the day.

"Are SOCiT involved yet? The Feds?"

"Not yet, I was considering it earlier today." I rubbed at my chin.

"Make the call, Jack." Hicks's voice had deepened.

I knew we'd need input from other departments, but so far, I'd resisted the idea. I couldn't say why, maybe the fact that I'd literally eaten, drunk and slept the case for the last few days might have had something to do with it.

Even if I had almost drunk myself to death and possibly lost my wife and children in the process, once I put the weasel responsible behind bars, I figured I'd feel some sense of satisfaction, a release. I just hoped it would be worth it, and at some point, Abbie would come back to me.

"So where are we at today?" Holmberg chimed in, bringing his chair closer and resting one elbow on the boardroom table.

"Next step, we search Marlin Jones's property. He's under arrest at present, so he shouldn't be too much of a problem." I flicked through the file containing photos of the crime scene.

"What are you thinking, Jack? If the current suspects aren't a DNA match, who's behind this?" Hicks continued pushing, but then she probably got daily calls from both the Regional Commander and the media unit for a story, ideally involving a resolution and an arrest, especially if my worst fears proved correct; a child serial killer.

"I'm getting closer to thinking there's a ringleader, and a network set-up, out of reach." There, I'd said it out loud.

"Like as in, a child trafficking ring?" Hicks's voice held a different tone, an undercurrent of warning, of danger.

"Possibly." Collen and Holmberg exchanged looks.

"Well, that confirms it, Jack. We're going to need to involve the Feds." She shoved her hands back in her pockets and walked around to stand beside me at the end of the table.

"Okay, I'd like to conduct the search of Marlin Jones' property first if I can." I didn't look at her. Instead, I began doodling on my notepad.

"No. You just make the call, Jack."

I looked to Collen and Holmberg for some help; maybe they'd back me up? But they simply blinked back at me, mute.

Damn.

"I will, I'll call the Feds and SOCiT." There was no point in fighting her on it; she was like a bulldog. Once she had a hold of something, there was no way she'd let go of it.

"Today, Jack, make the call today."

I didn't want to do it, but in the face of relentless pressure, I'd need to make a call. Hopefully, I'd be allocated someone with a reputation of being thorough, and not obstructive. Maybe I could talk to Collen and Holmberg after the meeting, find out who they'd recommend. Hopefully, someone who'd been around the block a few times. The last thing we needed was a fresh-faced newbie, filled with enthusiasm and the milk of human kindness.

Generally, newbies didn't have half a clue, yet their enthusiasm filled them with the idea it was all beer and skittles, all we'd need would be to follow the rule book to the letter, and everything would magically turn out all right.

None of us had the patience or the energy for a panting lap dog to tag along. Plus, the idea of the constant questions and explaining every time I had a brain fart didn't exactly thrill me.

Unless, of course, if they liked drinking whiskey until they fell unconscious around 4am. For that, I might be willing to make an exception.

CHAPTER SIXTEEN

I SIFTED THROUGH PAPERS on my desk, looking for the search warrant for Marlin Jones that had come back signed.

My phone buzzed with an internal call and I picked it up.

"Homicide. DS Fletcher speaking."

"Yeah, Jack, got a couple here at the front desk, pretty agitated. Melinda Holmes and her partner Eric. Asking for you. I told them you're doing everything you can, but they won't take no for an answer. I asked them to leave once, but they got more agitated."

"I'll come out to see them. Thanks, won't be long."

I slammed the phone down. Earlier that morning, I'd finally made the damn call to the Federal Police and SOCiT, and they'd been coordinating with me to execute the search warrant. The last thing I needed was dealing with Melinda Holmes and her histrionics.

Nevertheless, I pushed my chair back, and marched down the corridor, pushing open a door and then turning a corner until I found the entry to the front desk area. Melinda Holmes was red-faced, frowning and paced relentlessly in front of the helpless-looking sergeant.

"Melinda, DS Fletcher." I moved closer.

"About damn time. What the hell are you doing about finding the evil bastard that killed my little girl? I can't sleep. I won't rest until he's behind bars."

Eric, her boyfriend, placed one hand on her forearm, and she swatted it away.

"We're doing everything we can, I've just today made a couple of phone calls. Now we have more resources, I can assure you it won't be long until we find those responsible, and justice is done."

She snorted. "Justice! What a joke that is, I used to believe in our justice system once upon a time. Now I've lost my little girl, I have no faith at all. None! Do you hear me?" She dissolved into tears, and Eric resumed his position, placing his left arm around her shoulder and handing her a tissue.

I handed my card to Eric. "Feel free to call or email me at any time." I figured it might be easier to deal with her partner than Melinda herself, considering she seemed to vacillate between anger and grief fairly freely.

"Thanks," he said quietly. He took a step away and moved out of earshot of his girlfriend, who eventually sat down and commenced quietly sobbing into her tissue. "I'm sorry about this, but she's really in a bad way. I drove her over here only in the hope that it would calm her down, bring her some resolution, that's all. She doesn't usually make a scene, but as I'm sure you can understand..."

"I do, completely. I can't imagine what it's like to lose a daughter."

"Are you close to charging anyone for this yet? It would mean so much to both of us, bring some closure, some resolution, if such a thing is possible."

"I understand. We're considering all possibilities at present, but a couple of avenues are becoming clearer."

"Well, if you could keep us in the loop, we'd really appreciate it." Eric returned to stand beside Melinda, rubbing her back.

"As if he's going to call us? He spends most of his time sucking up to Will, why would he want to bother with us?" Melinda was back to anger, but then grief came in different forms. Unfortunately, at present, her grief was manifested in wildly alternating grief and belligerence.

Her outburst had begun to attract attention from various staff. "How about we make ourselves more comfortable in one of the interview rooms?" I looked at Eric, who made an attempt at a smile.

"That's a good idea," he said. "Come on honey, come with me, let's sit in here where it's a bit more comfortable." He attempted to steer her across, but Melinda Holmes was having none of it.

"Go away, you don't know what it's like, neither of you! My daughter's dead and never coming back. Do you hear me? Never! Some bastard stole her from me, and he gets to keep living his life, but my little girl is gone forever. What are you doing to find him? You still haven't answered my question, have you?" Her face contorted in grief, and tears rolled down her face.

"I can promise you I'm working flat-out investigating this, and I'm not working on any other cases at present. I won't stop until I know who did this, you have my word on that," I said.

"If you haven't found anyone yet, will you ever? They could be out there hurting other little girls, have you thought of that?" Melinda Holmes had screwed up her tissue, and Eric handed her a fresh one.

"Melinda, I'm confident we will find the person that did this. We don't have enough evidence to arrest the killer just yet, but I can tell you we have a couple of avenues of investigation that may lead us to him."

"Can't you use DNA?" she said. "If the sicko hurt my daughter did the unthinkable, he would have left DNA on my baby. That should lead you right to him."

I wasn't sure how to tell her that the person needed to be listed on the DNA database for us to find him, but I did my best. "We did find DNA, but if the person that did this isn't listed on the DNA register, it's difficult to track them down," I said.

"So, what does that mean? He'll just get away with this and never get found? How does that work? How is that fair?"

Eric made quiet noises meant to comfort his girlfriend, but she wasn't having any of it.

"No, it doesn't mean that at all. None of this makes sense, and none of it is *fair* either, but I'm working on the investigation night and day, you have my word on that," I said. I had to suppress the urge to say that me working around the clock and drinking myself into a stupor every night, nearly losing my job and already having lost my wife and kids wasn't exactly *fair* either. I breathed fast, annoyed but also understanding what they were suffering. I bit back the words I wanted to spit out.

To be honest, I wasn't sure if anything I could tell her would ease her pain or bring her comfort. I'd need to get started on executing the search warrant soon, as the Feds and team from SOCiT would be meeting me at Marlin's place at a pre-arranged time.

"You can spend all the time in the world on finding who did this, but doesn't mean it will ever happen does it?" she said, wiping at her face. She had now at least calmed down somewhat from screaming anger, to mild antagonism. I stooped to her level, resting on my haunches to see into her eyes. I meant this.

"I won't rest until I have answers," I said, looking from Melinda to Eric, and back to Melinda. She bowed her head. "Melinda. Look at me. I promise you."

"Well, then. Can you also promise me you'll call me when you have information. Or email Eric? That might be better," she said. "I am her mum, you know. It's not just Will that needs to know... And because we aren't together, Will doesn't tell me..." She seemed more upbeat now, despite the gripe at Will again; my words had reached her.

"Of course, I can. I'm sorry I haven't updated you before now, but once an investigation gets going, it changes quickly," I said. "And I didn't know Will didn't... you know." They nodded.

Eric pulled a piece of paper from his back pocket, while Melinda scrounged around in her handbag for a pen. He wrote on the piece of paper and handed it to me. "That's my email address; please email me if you have any information, no matter what, it will really help us," he said.

"I will, I'll let you know as soon as I have some information for you," I said.

Melinda hitched her bag up onto her shoulder and stood up. Eric placed one arm protectively around her shoulder. "Look, I'm sorry I made a scene, but it's all so fresh, so new, I don't know how to cope with any of this," she said, her voice much lower and softer than before. "I still expect her to walk into through the front door and throw her school bag on the floor. I can't believe she's really gone."

"I'm so sorry. I'll be in touch as soon as I can with any developments," I said. Eric made an attempt at a smile, and Melinda put her head down and headed for the main entrance.

As the doors slid open, both Melinda and Eric exited, and I let out a long breath.

An officer departed through the secure door to the offices and raised his eyebrows. "Tell me about it," I muttered.

For now, I'd need to talk to the Feds and SOCiT to coordinate the search warrant. After making myself a strong cup of coffee and making my way back to my desk, my phone rang, and I picked it up within two rings.

"Homicide, DS Jack Fletcher speaking."

"DS Fletcher, this is James Wells from SOCiT."

"Ah yes, I was just about to call."

"We have a search taking place under warrant shortly."

"We do."

"We have a team assembled and we're looking to meet you at the property in the next hour or so. That work for you, Jack?"

"Okay. Keep in mind it should all be fairly routine; the owner of the residence is currently in police custody."

"I see. That simplifies things quite a bit."

"Yeah; I need to speak to the Feds as they will have a presence during the search."

"The Feds are involved?"

"Suspected child trafficking ring, so I had to call them in. It was only a matter of time."

"I see. So, what time are we looking at?"

"Probably within the hour, so around 10 a.m. I think."

"Right, well I have your mobile number here. I'll give you a call when we're nearby."

"Okay, thanks."

I hung up. I clicked on an email I'd received, which contained a phone number for the liaison point with the Feds, Steve Wilcox. He had a specialisation in the area of child abuse and human trafficking.

Steve answered almost straight away. "Hello?"

"DS Jack Fletcher from crime command."

"I was just about to call you to coordinate times for this search warrant."

"I'm thinking around 10 a.m. SOCiT will have a small team there."

"Figures. What are we expecting, Jack?"

"Should be uneventful. The resident is currently in police custody, so we'll be left alone to do what we have to."

"Okay, good. I'll text you when I'm out the front. Can I have your mobile number please?"

I gave it to her, hung up, and got myself ready to leave.

With any luck, we'd find something, anything, to tie Marlin Jones to the crime.

Hopefully, we wouldn't have to release him anytime soon.

CHAPTER SEVENTEEN

THE TEMPERATURE HAD dropped a couple of degrees. It was cold as hell.

Grey clouds overshadowed patches of blue sky. I'd rugged up with three layers of clothing. I shoved my hands in my pockets and stood on the street outside Marlin Jones' home, somewhat detached from it all. I wondered if the search warrant would happen as easily as I'd convinced myself it would? It didn't matter how smooth or messily it went if we found the prize—namely, evidence to put Jessica's killer away.

Several unmarked vans were parked in the street, further down from Marlin Jones' home. We didn't bother parking further down from the house; we were right outside. Usually, we parked farther away so as not to alert the inhabitants, but in this case, with Jones locked up, it wasn't necessary. The core team members of Project Beacon crossed the street and headed my way, where I stood on the other side from Jones' home.

The search team amounted to Selena Hicks, Gary Holmberg, Larry Weston, Ed Garrett, Andy Collen, James Wells from SoCIT, and Steve Wilcox from the Feds along with Rae Swanson, as a courtesy.

We huddled together to coordinate before we conducted the search.

Our breath hung in the air in front of us, in plumes of mist.

"Okay, I'll go in through the front entrance. Rae and James, you take the rear. We don't anticipate any problems. The resident has been arrested for stalking, and he's in lockup. Hopefully, it'll be A to B. Let's make it quick and effective.'

"So, we're looking for anything that ties the resident to child murders?"

"Yeah, we're looking for laptops, computers, photos, weapons, evidence of children at the property, anything like that." I turned and nodded to Collen. "Let's go and get this over with; the sooner we get started, the sooner we can get out of here."

We moved and began walking towards the property. I hadn't taken my hands out of my pockets, telling myself this was nothing more than the next step in the process.

Somehow, I still hadn't fully convinced myself.

Garrett took one of the vehicles and drove it a short way, parking it just outside the place. It wasn't like anyone other than the neighbours had seen us arrive.

Marlin Jones's home was the same shithole as last time. Rae Swanson and James Wells headed down the driveway to position themselves at the rear and find a back entrance.

I paused at the front door with Collen, and Weston and Garrett on either side with weapons out. Although none of us voiced it, there could still be someone in there, no matter how remote the possibility. I shared a look with a Garrett. The screen door appeared to have been kicked open.

We counted down, looking one to the other. Although Jones wasn't home, he hadn't exactly given us a key, so Garrett stood a few steps back from the door, with a battering ram we fondly and informally referred to as *the key to the city*. The air was thick and still, not a trace of wind.

Strangely, at that moment I didn't hear a sound, no car doors slamming from neighbours, no birds, not a soul stirring.

"Okay," said Garrett. "On four, I'm ramming." We moved back away from the door.

He charged at the door; with an almighty bang, the wooden door splintered, and the frame snapped, followed by the door itself.

I kicked the last pieces of the door away and crossed the threshold. We were in.

One by one, we drew our weapons and cleared each room, just in case. Marlin may have rigged the house, and set it up to surprise us, but after a minute or two we all converged back in the hallway area.

"All clear," said Collen, brushing hair out of his eyes.

"Right, let's get moving. We're looking for photographs, weapons, fibres, anything that can tie this guy to the crime scene. Let's split up and take it room by room."

The first thing that greeted me was the stale, rotten smell. Obviously, housework was not high on Marlin's priority list. I moved rapidly through the rooms, scanning for anything that would help me press further charges against him.

Within minutes, Rae and James met up with me in the kitchen.

"Nothing," said Rae, hands on hips. "But maybe we're thinking like police officers, rather than criminals with something to hide. If I wanted to hide something, where would I stash it?"

I stormed back out towards the hallway, casting my gaze upwards. Towards the rear of the hall, a square hole appeared in the ceiling. It looked cleanish, a sign it may have been used recently—there was no dust on the hatch from what I could see. It was a possible entrance to an attic.

"Wells, Swanson—over here," I called out. "See if you can find a ladder, can you? If I was Jones, I'd use this as a hiding spot." I pointed up to the small square hole. Within minutes, a uniformed officer arrived with a ladder, and he set it up in the hallway.

"Want me to climb up, Sir?" he said.

"No thanks, want to check it myself." I checked the ladder was sturdy by placing both hands on either side of the frame and began the slow tentative climb upwards. The uniformed officer held the ladder in place at the base.

As I reached the hatch, I pushed it upwards, and it gave way fairly easily. I looked just inside and noticed a small light switch. I flicked it, and looking up, a bare lightbulb lit up. I pushed away from the entrance; towards the back of the attic, I thought I saw a small cardboard box hidden in a dark corner.

Shit.

I'd have to climb across the timber frames, avoiding the open, insulated sections so I didn't fall through the ceiling. I hunched over almost double in the cramped space and inched my way to the dark corner. I squatted carefully on the piece of timber, maybe 15 centimetres wide, and reached forward, feeling for the box. Breathing heavily in the stuffy space, my fingers found purchase and I pulled the box towards me. I lifted the

lid. In the dim light I saw what looked like three USB flash drives.

Bingo.

I squinted in the dark, and looked around for a laptop, or
similar device.

I saw what looked to be an old rag, about two feet away.
Holding onto a beam behind me, I tested my weight and
stretched out as far as I could with my left hand. I pulled at the
rag. I extended a hand and pulled at it to open up the rag.

Inside was a grey laptop. This had to be it. I dusted it off
and grabbed hold of both the cardboard box and the laptop.

Scanning the area again, I verified there was nothing else
hidden in the attic.

"Okay, I'm done up here. Found a couple of things. I'll pass
them down. Easy does it." I passed the laptop and the flash drives to Collen, next to Swanson and Wells who stood at the bottom of the ladder looking up.

"I'm heading down."

"Okay, Jack,"

I handed over the items and turned the light off in the
attic. I slowly backed down the ladder, eventually reaching solid ground, where I dusted myself off.

Rae Swanson appeared. "You found something?"

"Yeah laptop and a couple of USB sticks. I'm going to have
a look at them now while we're here. If he hid it in the attic, I
doubt it was something he wanted us to see."

I turned to Collen, who held the items out to me, and I
grabbed them and clomped down the stairs towards the front
porch, finding a couple of old chairs there. I sunk down into

one of them and opened up the laptop. Rae sat down in the chair beside me and leaned over for a closer look.

Surprisingly, there was no password. Opening it up, I went first to Explorer to search for images. Initially, there were what looked to be regular documents. As I clicked further, however, I saw a whole host of images. I clicked on the first and it appeared in a large view on the screen.

Prickles raced up my spine, and my stomach turned. These were no ordinary images.

Image after image contained children in various obscene poses, tied up, restrained, and in some cases dressed in various poses for the delight of the watcher.

I closed my eyes and paused for a moment before continuing.

"My God, this is it," whispered Rae.

This would certainly keep Marlin Jones behind bars for longer than anticipated. I'd need to take it back to the office and go through the entire laptop in greater detail for as long as I could stomach before handing it over to the e-crimes unit.

I closed the lid and sighed heavily.

"Are you taking this back to the office then?" said Rae.

"Yeah, I'll need to let the team know."

"I think I'll come with you. There's probably pictures of Louisa on there somewhere."

"I'm hoping this leads us to who's behind this. It's him I'm after."

Rae didn't reply. She stood up and went back inside to speak to the rest of the team. I paused for a moment, with the laptop under my arm and looked out into the street. This sicko had lived within walking distance of Jessica Holmes' house, with no requirement to list his details on a public sex offenders register.

The SOCiT team had been pushing for a national register for years, so at least families had some idea of who or what lurked in their neighbourhood, but in Australia, politicians weren't having a bar of it.

Further down the street, a group of children bounced a basketball at each other, laughing and joking. At least now—if nothing else—Marlin Jones was off the street and in custody, far away from where he could do harm to other children.

I'd make sure a healthy list of charges came his way, it was the least I could do until I'd found the bastard killing little girls.

I took a few steps from the porch back to the front door and walked back inside. The team was busily searching each room, opening cupboards and drawers. Collen was in the filthy bathroom, leaning into the medicine cabinet under the sink, where he was going through the contents.

"They should pay us danger money. Thank God I'm wearing gloves. Doesn't look like this joker cleaned this bathroom. Ever." Collen pushed hair out of his eyes and stood up straight.

"I've got enough to put Jones away for a long time. Pictures of young girls on the laptop, tied up, in various poses. I haven't gone through all of it yet."

Collen closed his eyes and opened them again after a moment. "Christ, are you up to going through all of that stuff?"

"Yeah. I'll hand it over to e-crimes when I'm done. Swanson and I are heading back to the office to get started, there's a lot to go through. Looks like they had a whole network set up."

"Okay, mate, well done. Well, I'll just finish up taking stock of this filth, and meet you there later." Collen went back to bagging some of the contents of the medicine cabinet. I didn't mention that the sick greasy feeling had returned to my gut, and I swallowed hard, forcing the nausea down.

I made my way towards my car, the wooden porch steps creaking as I stepped onto them. I'd almost reached the bottom when something brushed at my elbow and I turned.

James Wells from SOCiT stood at my side.

"Keep us updated," he said intently.

"Yeah, I'll go through these then pass them on to e-crimes. I'll call you and pass the information on to you and the Feds. There's a lot to go through."

"I heard," James voice sounded rough, guttural. "If it hasn't been said yet, well done. Don't need to tell you, you found something big today."

"Yeah," I said as James walked back inside the home. *Just not in time to save Jessica, Louisa, or the other two girls* I thought, shaking my head. My flesh crawled, and I wanted to take a shower after seeing some of the images. Jones had set them up, posed the children, dressed them in costumes, tied them up, and taken pictures for the sick pleasure of himself and others.

I'd need to go through some of the images before turning the laptop over to IT. The thought of it turned my stomach, but I needed to do it, as it could take me a step closer to what was really going on.

And I needed to talk to Jones, if he hadn't clammed up—or lawyered up—yet.

I trudged back to the car, trying hard not to think about what the young girls went through as the photos were taken.

CHAPTER EIGHTEEN

THAT NIGHT, KNOWING the nightmares would return, and to ease the loneliness of my empty house, I returned to my now constant old friend and companion, Mr. Jameson.

I'd stocked up, after getting over my denial about my return to the booze. I'd bought three bottles of my favourite whiskey. Jameson's, of course.

I knew I wouldn't get much sleep, although eventually I'd nodded off and gained a reprieve, blacking out for at least a few hours.

In the morning, with the early grey light, I showered, doused myself with mouthwash, and made my way into the office with the laptop under my arm, to begin the task of going through the images.

Swanson had sent me a text. *What time you in? Meet you at Crime Command 7.30?* She probably hadn't slept either. I met her in the underground car park around 7.30 a.m., both of us bleary-eyed.

"Couldn't sleep either, huh?" Her hands were shoved deep in her pockets, and the sockets around her eyes were pronounced, deep trenches having formed.

"Sleep is a luxury I can't afford on this job" I said. We both knew we were doing this for the little girls, the young victims with no voices. Hell, *we* were their voices, and I wouldn't rest until I found the sicko responsible.

I held the back door open to let her in.

We walked in silently, both walking towards the kitchen most likely thinking the same thing. Coffee.

Neither of us had the energy or inclination for small talk, so after we'd each poured a cup of black coffee, I walked out of the kitchen back to my desk, and pulled up an office chair, wheeling one across for Swanson. We sat at my desk. Only Jerry Wallace was in, and he looked as grim as we felt, giving us a serious nod, then turning back to his computer.

I slowly pulled the laptop from under my arm, shoved aside my keyboard, and stared at it, sitting it in the middle of my desk.

I thought about what I'd already seen, and what was there. For some reason, I paused. I'd come so far on the case, that now I was close to cracking it wide open, I wondered if I'd lost my nerve. Pretty pathetic for a detective of nearly twenty years.

You're weak as piss, Fletcher.

"Want me to start it up and start looking?" Swanson looked at me, waiting for an answer.

"You have kids yourself?"

"No, not yet, came close but..."

I had no idea what *came close* meant, but didn't really want to ask, it seemed far too personal a question. Instead, she answered it for me.

"Just finished with a guy. Four years."

"Relationships. Not easy, huh?"

"That's an understatement," she said quietly. We both stared at the laptop. Eventually, I pried the screen open and pressed the button in the left corner of the device. It made quiet whirring noises and the screen sprang to life.

We were in. I took a gamble and went to Gmail. Marlin Jones hadn't seemed like the sharpest tool in the shed when I'd interviewed him, and I had an idea.

Yep, there was his Gmail profile. I clicked on it and his password had been saved. It automatically filled itself in so I pushed *login*.

And there they were. Emails between Marlin Jones and his *buyer*s, judging by the subject titles.

I clicked on a recent one. It talked about transporting goods.

My heart pounded.

"How does this fit? Fill me in, Jack." Swanson rubbed a hand over her mouth.

"Confirms my theory. A child sex-trafficking ring. The sickest of the sick." I swallowed, hard.

"Who's involved?"

"So far, only the dead shit in custody, Marlin Jones. He has a record from years ago, sex with a minor. Not only was he at the park where Jessica was taken, but he lives on the same street as the family. Arrested him at the funeral for stalking, walking past like the pervert he is. Couldn't tie him to anything else, DNA on Jessica's body didn't match. But now, with this, this changes everything."

"So, what's your theory? Jones sought out the targets, brought them back to his place, then transported them to the killer?"

"Possibly. David McElroy's involved too, I know it. Sicko number two got called into the station after someone caught him in the public toilets. His orange van is on bank CCTV footage, where Jessica gets into his car. Same deal though, no DNA match. Whoever did the murders has never been charged with a crime before."

"Shit. So, Jones and McElroy are selling the girls to paedophiles." Swanson's face had paled slightly.

"Yeah, I'd say so. No proof they touched the girls, not that it matters as far as I'm concerned. They're just as guilty."

I clicked on another email. Maybe that way, I could work up to clicking on the images that lurked on the hard drive.

"Jack, got your text." Nikita Newhouse breezed past me, dressed in her usual gear. Orange shirt, green braces, cargo pants. She dropped her backpack on the floor and kicked it under the desk. "What we got?"

Swanson stared at her, and I realised I hadn't introduced her to the young woman we referred to as *the clown*. Not because she was comical, far from it, but because she dressed like a clown, although her skills extended to all things technological rather than gags.

"Sorry, this is Nikita Newhouse from e-crimes, IT."

She extended a hand to Rae, who shook it briefly. "Good to meet you," Newhouse said. "Niki is fine," she said.

Newhouse pulled an office chair over and rolled it across to sit next to us. "Heard we're looking for images and details to find the location of a child serial killer."

"Not sure that they'll make it that easy for us," I cleared my throat. "My theory is, this is a network. They're snatching girls, holding them, and loading the pictures up onto a website for sale to paedophiles. At some point, the children are murdered." I watched the lump form in Niki's throat.

"I see," she said. "Want me to take a look?" Niki extended a hand.

"Shortly. I wanted to scroll through the images, see if our two victims are there."

"Definitely," Swanson stood, pushed her chair back and folded her arms. "I need another coffee, I think."

"Might need something a bit stronger in this case," I said, but she'd already headed for the kitchen.

"Tell me about it," she muttered, without turning back.

My phone rang loudly. "Sorry, Niki, I'll need to take this."

"No problems," she said, lifting the strap of the purple backpack up and onto her shoulder. "You know where I am; give me a call when you're ready."

I swiped the screen. "Yeah?"

It was James Wells from SOCiT. I'd wondered how long it would take for him to want in on an update. Swanson arrived back with a steaming mug of coffee, her face drawn, and sat beside me. I was still on the phone with James.

"I've got the laptop powered up, just going through it now," I told him. "I'm here with Rae."

"Okay. What have you got?" James asked.

"Looks like Jones set up a buyer's network, probably via a website. They'd upload the images for buyers to look at, and then do the transfer."

James sucked in a large breath.

"Got an address of where they're holding the girls?"

"Not yet, I'm wading through it, there's a tonne of information on here. If I get an address, I'll let you and the Feds know straight away."

"Okay Jack, good lad. Thanks." James hung up.

I turned to look at Swanson. The colour had returned to her face.

"You ready to do this?"

"As ready as I'll ever be," she said quietly.

"The IT woman left?" Swanson warmed her hands on the coffee cup and brought it up to take a sip.

"Yeah, I told her we wanted to take a look first, I'll turn it over to her once we're finished. She can probably find out the website details, which are probably encrypted."

I removed the first USB drive from the box, plugged it in, and clicked on a folder. The images appeared one by one. Images of miserable little girls in various poses, bound, and dressed up in a series or costumes for the pleasure of grown men.

"Oh, my God," breathed Swanson.

Pictures of young girls I didn't recognise flashed up. Girls the same age as Jessica, and in some cases, even younger.

"I don't see Louisa," said Swanson, scanning the images.

"Me neither."

My stomach dropped, and my throat ached. Without warning, there was Jessica Holmes, tied up, wearing a tiny, horrendously incongruous French maid's outfit, sitting on a bed. Her eyes were wide in terror.

"Keep clicking on the images, Jack, don't dwell on them. Easier said than done I know but keep going."

I clicked on the next few. There were so many girls, no boys that I could see at all. Then my heart lurched. Louisa Fein appeared, and Swanson covered her face with her hands. She let out a gasp. Louisa had been bound in leather straps at both the hands and feet, and was dressed in a frilly pink dress, with far too much makeup plastered across her face. She lay on a bed, her miserable face telling the story.

"If only I'd got to her earlier, she would have lived." Swanson lifted her face, to stare again at the image.

"I know that feeling, Swanson, but we can't let it eat us alive. There's a way we can fix this—by finding an address, and if any girls are still alive, get 'em out of wherever they're being held."

Swanson let out a breath, unable to speak for the moment. I watched as her face changed colour again from pasty white, to pink, to scarlet, and she clenched her fists.

"Let's get these bastards and find those girls. Open up the email program again Jack, they have to be holding them somewhere." Her voice sounded deep and filled with a quiet fury, a fury I knew only too well, one that had become endless nights filled with nightmares, stopped temporarily—at least in my case—only by copious bottles of whiskey.

"Okay," I shut down the window of the countless images of little girls being held against their will. I opened up the email to scour the emails Marlin had sent to several anonymous receivers. Scanning the subject titles, one of them jumped out of me. The heading read, *Transport of goods.*

That had to be it. Swanson sat up straighter in her chair and pointed. "That's it, Jack, we've got them. That's got to be it!"

I opened up the email. It detailed a transfer of goods to a location in Melbourne, a few kilometres from the city. Date of delivery was Wednesday March 24th, the next day at 10 a.m.

I grabbed my phone and found James' number. "We'll need backup," Swanson said but she was already up and out of her seat. She began pacing. "Give me a few seconds to set this up, then we'll get moving."

James picked up within just two rings. "We've got an address." James sounded as pleased as we were,

"In the email?"

"So, when and where?"

"Let me talk to the boss first, we might need to meet here to coordinate before we swarm the place and get any kids out. There may be no kids there, we don't know."

"What does the email say?"

"Delivery of goods tomorrow at 10 a.m."

"Shit."

"Let me talk to Hicks, and we'll take it from there."

"Okay, stay in touch. And stay frosty."

"Come on Jack, let's go!" Swanson had moved down the corridor that led the back door.

"We can't just show up, it has to be coordinated."

She paused, head turned, a frown crossing her face. "What? We have an address. There could be children there now, held in God only knows what conditions. We have to help them."

"I get it, but this is a task force now, we can't go off half-cocked. Come on, I'll ring boss lady, then we'll talk."

Swanson swore, blew out a long breath, then stormed back down the corridor and sat back down. She knew as well as I did we had to play it by the book, but I understood the emotion pulling her towards the location. I'd never tell another soul, not even Garrett, Collen, Holmberg—hell, not even my wife—that so far, this job had made me cry a whole lot of times.

I pulled out my phone and rang Selena Hicks.

"Jack."

"We went through the laptop. They're talking in code, *delivery of goods tomorrow*, it says in an email. Hundreds of sick photos, all little girls."

Hicks didn't answer so I continued, repeating some of what we'd found a second time. "Jones sent an email about delivery of goods and gives an address."

"So, the goods are the children." Hicks' voice was quiet and low.

"Girls, yeah. We have the address, delivery happens 10 a.m. tomorrow."

Another pause. "Let's notify the Project Beacon team. It's 5 p.m. now. We'll coordinate in the briefing room at 7 p.m. before we head out. We'll check the place out. They could be holding girls there right now. See you then."

I hung up. Swanson stared at me. "Well?"

"We notify the Project Beacon team. Meet in the briefing room at seven."

"That's two hours away." Swanson sat forward in the chair, hands balled into fists.

"Look, I need to call the team. Then maybe we could grab something to eat."

"Eat? *Seriously*?"

I had a bitter tang on my tongue, my throat burned, and my stomach heaved. "Yeah I know, but who knows when we'll get a chance to go out and eat again."

"Let's start calling." Swanson had her phone out.

"Jack, hold on." Wallace turned from his desk a few metres away. "You didn't think you'd get to have all the fun without me, did you? You'll need backup, I've called for it; they'll meet us in the briefing room. You might also need an ambulance if the girls are injured, consider it done."

"Great."

"Thanks, mate, SOCiT will meet us here in a couple of hours."

"Right," he said.

It was game on.

CHAPTER NINETEEN

PROJECT BEACON HAD hit full swing. We needed to move fast before the media got wind of the swoop on the address, 16 Calcutta Street, Footscray. The suburb itself had become a melting pot with hipsters and young urban professionals moving in over recent years, but the elements of drug dealers, prostitutes and crime lingered.

Before we hit the address, boss lady had suggested a meeting, so here we all were at 7 p.m. Tuesday, the night before the supposed delivery at 10 a.m. Thursday.

Eight officers, James Wells from SoCIT and Rae Swanson, Steve Wilcox from Federal Police, plus Hicks, Holmberg, Garrett, Collen, Wallace, Weston—and myself—filled the briefing room. The doors were closed, and the projector screen on. Armed with coffee, we milled around until boss lady kicked the meeting off.

"Okay folks, this is it. As many of you know, we have a laptop, belonging to Marlin Jones who is currently in custody. We have photos of little girls in compromising positions and what looks to be a child network ring. The girls are sold, abused, and in some cases murdered. An email sent between Jones and an unknown person mentions a *delivery* tomorrow at 10 a.m.

We're heading in tonight to search the premises. Prepare your-selves. There may be young girls in God knows what condition, held captive, and suspects on the premises."

"So, we're going in to rescue girls potentially tonight. How about tomorrow?" Asked Holmberg.

"Like any search operation, we're unsure of what we'll be faced with. We'll remove any children from the property and transport them to safety, as well as adults, until they are cleared. Tomorrow morning, depending on what we find, either us or the special operations group sweep the place." Hicks said.

Although I still felt sick, adrenaline surged. This was it. I might get my hands on the sick twisted fucker that did this.

"It goes without saying to take care everyone; while this isn't our first time around the block, we have no idea what we're headed into. Logistics-wise, our armed officers will secure the front entrance," said Hicks, fully kitted up.

"Fletcher and Collen, take the back. Holmberg and Gar-rett, check the fence and boundary." I said. My heart pounded, and I hoped to hell my voice hadn't wavered. I'd kept it low, quiet and as even as possible.

Plans of the property flicked up on the screen. "And the basement?" Asked Weston.

Swanson stepped forward. "I can cover that," she said.

"Okay, let's do this. If there are children in there, let's get them out safely." The huddle dispersed. "Fletcher, Collen, Gar-rett, we'll go together," Hicks said.

Boss lady and I headed straight for the car park. She frowned so hard her eyebrows threatened to shadow her eyes. No one spoke. We got to her black Falcon. With a beep, it un-locked.

Garrett and Collen got in and sat in the back, while boss lady and I took the front.

"We got this," Collen didn't look at me, his voice a steel edge. Hicks started up the car, turning her head around to reverse the vehicle. She swung the steering wheel in one fluid action, gunning the accelerator.

I didn't answer, my body rolling with the car and my mind focussing on the cars in front of us at the traffic lights, thinking about the end goal. And that goal was arresting the piece of shit that raped, tortured and killed little girls for kicks.

Hicks flicked on the siren, and eventually the light went green and we took off. I cast a look across and noticed Selena Hicks's left jaw flickering, most likely also thinking about our faceless enemy. We hit three lanes, then the main road.

The drive took no more than twenty minutes. We turned into a road on the right. Cars packed the narrow street, one marked Federal, an unmarked car for SoCIT, and two squad cars.

I was out of the car in seconds, but Hicks was already out, and she slammed the door shut, sighing as she shoved both hands on her waist. She looked about and we huddled around her. The Feds and SoCIT had messaged me on the way.

I planted my feet, directly facing her. Garrett, Collen, and three uniformed officers huddled up to my right and left. "Right, let's go. Let's take this as professionally and calmly as we can," said Hicks.

I hadn't seen her like this for a long time, her mood balancing on a knife edge, threatening to teeter into full-blown fury.

Hicks frowned.

James Wells from SOCiT walked over, hands in pockets, grey-haired and clean-shaven. "Evening," he said, staring at the ground. He stood between Hicks and Garrett. "Ready to go?"

"Yep" Hicks pivoted on one foot. Hicks' silent fury was more dispersed tonight with deep breaths, and her closed eyes had narrowed into a thick dark line.

Drawn to her energy, we followed behind her, taking strength from a common purpose. Just as we'd been briefed to do before we'd set off, Collen and I crept around the overgrown garden as shadows slowly moved across it, heading to the back door.

Holmberg and Garrett had already made for the back fence, and were about fifty feet away, almost obscured by bushes and trees, with weapons drawn. Two other officers scanned the windows; that way, the scumbags had nowhere to run. Swanson couldn't be seen. I had no doubt she was hanging back until given the go-ahead to rush forward and scan the basement, once we were in.

As usual, my heart rate had gone up, chest pounding and blood flowing speeding through my veins. I took heavy gasps outside the back door, on one side of the door, with my weapon drawn, and Collen had his drawn on the opposite side. Swanson stood behind om me now, weapon in the raised position. She had made it to the back door and wanted to be inside, searching.

I took a second to slow my breathing, and focussed on her.

With an almost unnoticeable nod of the head, I tried the old-fashioned metal door handle knob, but of course it was locked. I took a couple of steps back, and thought of Jessica Holmes, her body in Sherbrooke forest, her family. I offered up a silent prayer as I slammed my body weight against the door and it gave way.

This one's for you, Jessica. We'll get the man that did this, I promise.

Entering through the smashed-open door, a stench wafted into my face, a combination of urine, stale decomposing food and dead animal.

I turned with my firearm out, ducking through a doorway to my right, with Collen right behind me and Swanson went straight ahead through to the basement.

Through another doorway, a painted white wooden stairway curled downwards to my right. I lowered the weapon in my right hand and indicated to Swanson, and Collen silently, motioning with my other hand. The stairs descended into the darkness. Hell, I wanted to get down there myself, but it was Swanson's assigned tasking. I held my breath until I thought I would pass out. Swanson lurched forward, her own firearm held forward. "Police!" she cried. "I am armed, lie down on the ground!"

I didn't hear anything. Just a quiet echo.

Steps creaked as she went. The staircase took a U-turn and she was enveloped in darkness. The stuffiness down there had increase. It seemed such a long time.

My stomach curdled. I slowly crept down after her—what was the sense in waiting at the top? She needed backup. I walked down until I was a step behind her. Four narrow stairs lead off sideways, to a dark landing. I pulled a pen flashlight from my jacket pocket, motioning to Swanson that I would take the staircase down to the landing to my right. She nodded, silent.

The door was stuck, and I tested it with my body weight before it gave way. I swung the flashlight around and my stomach almost heaved. The stench assaulted me like a hard slap to the face, the stench of human waste, of pent-up bodies in small, stifling cavities, and of blood, sweat, and vomit. Then, illuminated before us, were emaciated children with sticky hair and dirty faces as they stared wild-eyed.

Weak groans and gasps filled the air. The children began calling and wailing in a language I didn't recognise. I crouched down to their level, and my knees cracked.

"It's okay, girls, you're safe." The girls babbled louder, some of them standing up and screaming at full volume.

A dark-haired girl to my right screamed, a bloodcurdling scream that set my teeth on edge. I put my weapon away, back in its holster.

I extended a hand towards her slowly and gently, but she screamed louder so I stood up slowly and backed away. From the moonlight streaming into a dirty window with metal bars across it I saw a metal bucket in the corner, filled with faeces and urine. But one bucket was nowhere near enough for this many children. I stepped around faecal matter, fluids and vomit as I went.

I heard footsteps and turned toward the stairway. Swanson descended quietly toward me now, speeding up her pace as she reached the bottom of the four small stairs. She crouched down and approached the girls too, smoothing down one girl's hair, whispering, "It's okay now, honey, it's okay."

I grabbed the phone and called James Wells from SOCiT. "James, the girls are down here, in the basement."

"OK we'll send the paramedics in; the ambulance was on alert, it's less than a minute away."

The rest of the girls now wept and screamed quietly, their energy spent. I barely noticed the two officers filing down the stairs behind me. They paused as the girls screamed louder. We got the cages open to release the girls. Swanson stood up and hugged three of the girls close to her body as they sobbed into her arms. The others joined them, huddled in a circle of misery.

I walked back up the first set of stairs, entering a trance-like state, cut off, numb. At the top of the second set of stairs, James Wells from SOCiT stopped me. "The ambulance is here. They'll be okay now, Jack."

I barely heard him, nodding on autopilot, and continuing cutting a path to the front of the house; I turned right at a doorway just after reaching the main floor, and paused in the filthy kitchen. Someone touched my left shoulder, and I looked up.

Collen and Holmberg. Neither of them smiled. "Did well, Jack," said Holmberg said. "Another one to you."

"Jessica's still dead no matter what happened here today," I said, my voice low. I felt sad, deflated.

"We saved lives, that means something," he said.

"I guess," I mumbled and continued walking towards the front of the house. I needed air. Holmberg didn't follow. I was glad.

I figured I should wait for the ambulance, make sure the girls were okay, but the sick feeling had returned, along with a pounding headache. I opened the front door to Selena Hicks, and with the tilt of a chin, she indicated for me to meet her outside.

I stood in the long grass in the pathetic mixture of old concrete, dying plants and shadows. Hicks shuffled her feet.

"We got the girls, but not the sickos who did this," she said.

"Yeah. Close, but not close enough. In my book, that's a fail."

Hicks sighed as if irritated. "Look. I get it, Jack, but seriously... Enough of this shit now. You want to beat yourself up over it, I get it, but we don't all want to wallow in your continual misery. Some jobs affect us more than others—and it's what we signed up to, goes with the job. But it's affecting your ability to find the killer. So, stop with the self-pity and recriminations, and crack on. Either us or another team will be back here in the morning to arrest the sickos."

I spun to my right. "Okay, whatever. I've had enough for one night."

A flurry of activity interrupted us, a barrage of footsteps coming down the concrete steps behind me, and a series of paramedics with bags, moving up and down the driveway.

Holmberg, Garrett and Collen joined Hicks and me outside.

"The media will get wind of this soon enough. I better alert the Media Unit," Hicks said as she pulled out her phone and dialled a number, walking away a few steps as the call connected.

The top of Swanson's head appeared first, whispering to a dark-haired wraith of a girl, and as she walked out into the light of the front porch, she stared at me with dull unseeing eyes. Swanson held the girl's right hand in her left, escorting her towards the ambulance.

A paramedic with sandy hair appeared to my left, along the driveway where the ambulance was parked. He strolled along the footpath and walked towards the girl. A stream of dishevelled young females appeared behind her, walking beside officers. They came down the concrete steps and into the waiting arms of paramedics and female uniformed officers.

Sandy Hair extended a hand to the screaming girl I remembered from the basement, and she nervously took it. Swanson followed behind them both, and as she walked to the ambulance, my gut twisted, stabbing shards of glass driving up and into my chest.

I swallowed, hard.

This time, the burning tears fell unchecked, as I watched the paramedics help the little girls up and into the vehicle, its engine running and ready to take them to safety, cuddles and a hot bath.

CHAPTER TWENTY

AFTER THE GIRLS WERE loaded into the ambulance, I high-tailed it out of there. James Wells from SoCIT informed me a female SoCIT officer would stay with the girls in the hospital, where they'd liaise with the Department of Human Services regarding foster care for the children.

Collen, Garrett and Holmberg, as expected, shook my hand before I left.

Hicks wanted a debrief but that would come tomorrow after the Special Operations Group had set up surveillance at the property during the proposed 10 a.m. delivery of goods, to see if anyone showed up. I'd talked to Hicks about it, and pushed to go back there the next morning to potentially arrest the sickos myself, but Hicks had called in Special Operations Group (SOG) for the potential arrest.

"We're off to Ed's place for a drink. We've got a cold one with your name on it." Holmberg leaned on one of his hips.

"No thanks mate, might head off."

I watched the back of Ed's navy-blue wind jacket as he walked away down the driveway deep in thought, most likely headed for his car.

I needed some space. I shoved my hands in my pockets and looked up at the clear sky, stars sprinkled across the sky. I stared up at the stars, locating the Southern Cross constellation, and immediately felt small and insignificant.

With a sigh, I walked down the driveway and along the street, relief washing over me. The girls were safe now.

I'd taken about ten steps when a car pulled up beside me. Lifting my head, I saw Ed's car. The window whirred as it went down, and I bent at the knees, to see his scraggy face at the wheel.

"Get in."

"Thanks mate, but I need a walk."

"To where? Your car isn't here. Get in, mate, it's okay." He sounded calm and quiet. I opened the door and got in. Ed flicked on the car's indicator and slowly accelerated. Hunters and Collectors' *Throw Your Arms Around Me* played on the stereo.

I missed Abbie and my kids. I ached for a hug from my wife.

Ed's navy-blue car cruised along the street, where neglected houses and lawns stood silently in the darkness. He turned right at the corner. I sat in silence, letting the inky night surround me. It felt good to feel small and unimportant in the grand scheme of things. These stars weren't going anywhere.

Thirst burned my throat.

"Riley's Hotel on Footscray Road?" Ed tilted his chin.

"You read my mind." I hadn't really planned my destination, but it was a minute or two away. From there, I could either crash at the hotel, or get a taxi to my lonely home.

The hotel it was.

We'd reached Rivetts Road, shops and restaurants dotted along it. We pulled up at a red light, and two druggies crossed the road, dark circles under their eyes, one of them with purple hair, and the other with more piercings than a voodoo doll.

"We saved the lives of innocent girls tonight." Ed turned to look at me, hands still on the wheel.

"Maybe, but I can't forget a serial killer is out there some-where. A kid killer." I rubbed my upper lip with my right fore-finger.

"It's only a matter of time, mate, we both know that." Ed hit the gas and we took off slowly. At this hour, there were only a few people around. As he turned right onto Footscray Road, people walked up and down, and more lights were on, mainly in Asian restaurants and hotels, large and small.

Ed pulled up in front of a lane way. The lights for Riley's Hotel were about fifty metres away, and I watched as a couple of blokes walked in.

"Thanks." I opened the passenger door. Ed dropped his left hand on my shoulder.

"Take care. We're all in this."

"Yeah." I closed the car door and headed for the entrance.

Surprisingly, the public bar next door wasn't that busy, but then it was Tuesday night.

Surprisingly, Rae Swanson appeared at the black leather bar stool to my right, sliding her rump silently beside me.

Joe the barman finished pouring a beer and headed over.

After Swanson had ordered her drink, and taken her first sip, I broke the silence.

"It's a special occasion. I'm drinking in a bar."

I didn't turn to face her. From the corner of my eye, I saw her take a couple of long swigs.

She put the empty glass down on the counter top. "I didn't sign up for this shit. That girl..."

I rested my elbows on the bar and took another sip of Johnny Walker. "Yeah."

She leaned her left elbow on the shiny dark wood. "I need a shower," she said, sniffing at her clothes.

"God knows where her parents are. Some of them sounded like they spoke Russian," I said.

"Her screams..." Swanson said.

"Nice drop." It was all I could think of to say. Time passed. We passed it. In silence. Together.

Suddenly, Swanson yanked the lapel of her jacket to an inch from her nose and screwed up her face again. The silence, the contemplation, the drink. None of it worked to even begin to rest the torment inside our heads. We'd been stupid to think that it could.

"I hate to think how long those girls were there. The stench was something else." she rubbed her forehead, then sighed.

"Didn't see any rats but it wouldn't surprise me." I screwed my eyes shut, hoping the image of that dark, dank basement would disappear in time.

"SoCIT will see them right; they'll get counselling, go to good homes," I said, knowing how the latter part of my statement made them sound like abandoned cats or dogs.

Where the hell were their parents?

"The sicko that did this is still on the loose!" I could barely get the words out. I hung my head, staring at the swirling tornado of amber liquid in the glass.

"The girls are free now," Swanson said.

I turned to face her. "Free? You think that with all this shit inside their minds, they'll ever be free?"

She just looked at me and rested a hand on my forearm. "Hey. You know what I meant," she said, softly. "And the answer's no."

"We need to nail the scumbags," I said. Nothing had changed. Not a thing. Yes, we found the girls. But it was far from over, for any of us.

"The buyer is the key." Swanson shuffled forward on her stool and pulled one leg up across the other.

"That fucking buyer's out there somewhere, paying for the kidnapping of little girls, running his sick twisted network, piling up the cash. Murdering innocents without a second thought." I rubbed my eyes with the heels of my hands.

I didn't flinch at Swanson's hand again, warm on my shoulder.

"We'll find him, Jack." I raised my head. Her hazel eyes were flecked with green.

"In the time I've been sitting here, they could have killed another little girl. Someone's daughter, someone's sister." The image of my daughter pushed its way in, my Maddy, playing on the swings with her sister. In the same park.

I sat up straight and took a deep breath.

"Don't be so hard on yourself. You saved the lives of dozens of girls tonight. You did that. We all did. You could've given up, but you didn't."

"I had no choice. I won't sleep properly until I find this guy." I picked up my glass, swirling the last of the drink around in the bottom, debating whether to finish it off.

"Tomorrow is a new day." I wondered if Rae Swanson was talking to me now, or to herself. Probably both.

I finished off the last of my drink, wondering if tonight I'd get some sleep.

"I'm off," I said as I flicked a glance at Swanson. I stood up, intending to head for the front desk to get a room.

Swanson touched my shoulder. "Jack, we saved lives tonight. We will find the killer."

I looked back at her. "Yeah. Right. Okay."

I sounded angry. I sounded dismissive and downright fucking rude. And I didn't even care. I left her standing there, looking at my back as I walked away. I walked around a table of patrons, and cold air wafted across my face as I opened the main door. I took a step outside onto the street and spied a sign to my left for the main hotel, rather than the public bar.

A horn honked, and a couple walked towards me, arm in arm, faces aglow.

The hotel reception area was quiet and warm. The dark-haired receptionist greeted me with a smile. "Hello, how can I help?"

"A single room for the night please."

"Of course."

After handing over my credit card and driver's license, I took the key and headed to the lift. Once in my room, I pulled out my phone and called Abbie.

She answered on the third ring. "Jack?"

"Abbie, thanks for picking up."

A pause.

"I guess I've had some time to think," she said. I sighed in relief. She was going to come home. We could be a family again. I wanted to cry. But couldn't. I was numb.

"Me too," I said, my voice faltering. I kicked off my shoes and propped my right arm behind my head, lying down on the bed. "I'm sorry, Abbie. I neglected you and the girls, took you for granted, especially on this job. No excuses."

Another pause. "I get it, Jack, I really do, I've been a police wife for years. But something is different this time, you know?"

"Yeah I think I do. I can't tell you how sorry I am."

"Thank you, but let's not do *sorry*, okay? Let's just be civil with each other, that would be a good start."

"Yeah." A pause. "It's almost over, Abbie, we saved some little girls' lives tonight." She didn't respond; she didn't want to hear about my work.

"Speaking of girls..." she said. My chest caved in. My daughters. Abbie's voice became breathy. Then I heard the creak of a door opening. "It's Daddy," Abbie said.

The squealing of my youngest, Maddy, pierced the phone line. I tried to swallow but my throat seemed to have blocked up.

"Daddy!" she nearly blew my head off with the pitch and volume.

"Maddy. I've missed you, honey. So much."

"Well," she said, sounding indignant like only a little girl could. "Where have you been, Daddy? When can I see you?" Ah, so much like her mother already. I smiled broadly, the first in a long time. My eyes stung.

"Well, honey, I've been working." My voice cracked and wobbled. I took a deep breath and sat up. "I might see you Sunday but I need to talk to Mum first." *Careful Jack, don't make promises you can't keep.*

"Yay! Daddy! I got seventy percent on my maths test." I imagined her, eyes shining, out of breath, arms wide. Her beautiful long hair would be out of her school ponytail by now, the honey blonde hair streaked with natural gold and smelling divine, like fresh laundry.

The same hair Jessica Holmes had... hers had probably even smelled as good, to Will Holmes. But her hair no longer contained life. I wondered if Will Holmes took a lock of it at the funeral? I had to snap myself back to the chat with my daughter; one second, I'd been beaming. Now, I was back at Crime Command yet again. I could have beaten my head against the wall, angry at myself.

Another deep breath. "Daddy?"

Back to reality. "Sorry honey, I'm tired. Well done, you're so clever."

She giggled. "I'm talking, stop!" A rustling, then the phone was taken away from her. The soothing tones of Abbie came on, playing peacemaker. Then she handed the phone back to an impatient Maddy, who had more to say.

"Well, Daddy. I need you to be at home more. Why are you always away?"

"Maddy, honey. It's just work. I'm spending a lot a time on the job. That's why I'm hardly home, so... But I do think of you all the—"

"Daddy?" she interrupted.

"Yes, honeybun?"

"Are you and Mummy splitting up?"

I recoiled.

I leaned forward and ran my fingers through my hair. "No, there's a lot of pressure with this job, that's all. It's been on the TV."

"Were you on TV?"

"I was, yes, a few days ago."

"Cool!"

"Mummy and I are not splitting up. I'll probably see you soon, okay? Can you put Mummy on, so we can work it out please?"

"Yep. See ya Daddy."

Another sigh. I fell back on the bed.

"I'm here." Abbie sighed. She sounded stressed now, less lighthearted than at the start of the call. I'd definitely underestimated the pressure that running a family alone could put on a woman.

"Thank you. I mean it," I said.

"I know you do. But one step at a time, okay?"

"Okay, agreed. I'm sorry. This time, it's been...intense."

A sigh, an intake of breath.

"Well, one thing I never doubted was your ability to do your job," she said. There was a pause. It felt warmer, though, somehow. I heard Abbie breathing, hard.

"Jack?" she said, making sure I would listen to what was coming next.

"Yes?"

"Well d... I mean, *well done*."

The tears started to flow. I had to keep a grip. "Well done...for what?" I hoped she couldn't hear that the big man was in pieces and his shoulders were quivering, ready to break down.

"Just for... just for everything you are doing and everything you have achieved," she said. She meant it. I could tell.

"You don't even know about it yet," I said, gently. I tried to sound as if I was laughing, just a little. But she would know I was thankful for her words and how much they meant.

"And I don't need to know, Jack. You see, I know *you*. I know how hard you work so it will have had results. So, well done. That's all."

I took a massive inhalation to stop the tears from coming, just like trying to hold back a sneeze. I pinched my arm to focus on the pain instead.

"Thank you. Thank you... Abbie, thank..." I trailed off. It was enough. It was all I could say, anyway. My throat hurt from holding in tears.

We were definitely moving in the right direction, so I breathed in again, pushed a little. I was scared. My heart was in my mouth.

"Do you think I could see the girls sometime soon? I mean, not if you don't think... It's your call."

"I think that's a definite possibility, they miss you too, you know." My chest lurched. I imagined a cuddle with my daughters, remembered happier days, me lying on the couch at home exhausted and how they'd both run into my arms. I'd kiss their tiny heads and hold them tight, smoothing down their hair.

"Thank you. We rescued some little girls today," I told her, again.

"Oh, Jack," Abbie breathed into her phone. Oblivious to background noise earlier, I heard music and shuffling noises, possibly Maddy's big sister.

My eyes stung again, and my face and arms flushed with heat. "Anyway, enough shop talk. How's everything going at your sister's place?"

"Okay," Abbie obviously didn't want to give too much away, in case her sister heard. "Well, you know."

"She's there right? Say no more. I'd love to see the girls, and grab a coffee? How about Sunday?" This was only five days away. I wondered if the case would be wrapped up by then. Maybe that way I wouldn't even need to use breath spray to cover my alcohol breath.

"Let's do that. I'll text you where and when."

Obviously, I wouldn't want to meet up at my sister-in-law's place, but a bit of neutrality wouldn't hurt. The last thing I wanted was a fire-breathing sister on the war path on her own territory.

"Thanks, Abbie."

"It's okay. I'll text you soon."

"Okay. Bye."

"Goodnight, Jack." her voice sounded lower, quieter.

She hung up.

I got up and looked out through the window at the lights below. Things were looking up. I might get to see my girls again.

I had a chance. This time, I wouldn't blow it.

Swanson was right. Tomorrow would be a new day.

I'd find the piece of shit that did this.

I'm coming for you, you fucking dirt bag.

CHAPTER TWENTY-ONE

I ARRIVED IN THE OFFICE at 7 a.m. At least the Jessica Holmes nightmares had stopped, although the haunting face of the unnamed girl from the basement swirled around in my head before sleep. She was staring at me with round, dark eyes set back into a dirty face, her black hair hanging in rats' tails. We'd made eye contact only briefly before she looked up at Swanson, who'd wrapped a protective arm around her, and squatted down to whisper sounds of comfort in her ear.

Swanson. She'd been in my dreams too, along with the girl, which was slightly disconcerting. I'd never dreamed about Holmberg or Garrett, nor about my buddy Collen, nor Selena Hicks.

Around 8 a.m., the noise level increased as more personnel arrived, filling up all three of the cubicles in my quarter. Holmberg, Garrett, Wallace and James from SoCIT made an appearance briefly.

They offered an obligatory grunt, but I replied only with a nod.

Turning back to my cubicle, I continued my work. I'd fired up the laptop early and begun combing through the thousands of emails on Marlin Jones' filthy laptop. I'd spent over an hour going through them already. A pattern had emerged, with thousands of contacts, but none of them buyers. Emails discussed the weather, or what they were eating, but nothing about the so-called *goods*.

It was all in fucking code.

I figured the prick had deleted the meaty stuff, where the real criminal activity occurred. It was time to call in the IT nerd again, Niki. My mobile phone was on the desk, and it vibrated. I picked it up.

A text from Swanson. *What's on for today?* It read.

I pressed reply and sent her a text back. *Trawling through emails, plus a visit to Marlin Jones. I'll keep you in the loop.*

Next, I hit *new SMS* and sent a message to Niki the IT consultant. *Please trace deleted emails ASAP. Project Beacon.*

That should do it.

Garrett sat at the desk next to me and swivelled his chair around to my direction. "What's the latest, mate?"

I cleared my throat and turned my own chair around to look at him. Rather than bags under his eyes, Garrett had suitcases and deep-shadowed crevices. He'd shaved, and wore a clean shirt, light blue. "Going through these emails sent by Jones. There's thousands."

"No trace, huh?"

"Prick seems stupid, but there's no record of any buyers, no purchases of what he calls *goods* at all. All deleted."

Garrett swore under his breath.

"What about Niki in IT? She's onto it?"

"Sent her a text a few minutes ago, should be here soon."

"Did someone say my name? In a good way, gentlemen, though... I'm sure." Nikita Newhouse, Niki to us, wore a bright red shirt and a white all-in-one, jeans attached to an apron and straps. Her smile, as usual, beamed throughout the room and she looked at both of us, hands in pockets.

I managed a thin smile. "I'll get the laptop for you now." I turned back towards my desk. Ed Garrett watched the goings-on.

I unplugged the cords from the laptop, picked it up and turned to my right to give it to Niki.

"Over here, Jack," I turned in the direction of Niki's voice, where she'd now moved around to stand at the other side of my desk, to the left of my chair. "So basically, an undelete service for emails?"

"Yeah." My temperature seemed to have rocketed up a degree or two. "Laptop belongs to a paedophile by the name of Marlin Jones."

I looked up at her. She frowned as she took the laptop and tucked it under her arm. "Anything else?"

I wasn't keen on telling her too much more, although obviously she worked in Melbourne Crime Command. I couldn't shake the fact that she was not only a woman, but young, not that I'd ever admit either of those things being a factor.

"I'm looking for emails mentioning either transport or purchase of *goods* and the identity of the sender." Collen rubbed his hands down his trouser legs, cleared his throat then turned back to his computer screen.

"Okay, got it. I'll have this back to you ASAP." Niki's frown remained, and she walked away, head down.

I took a deep breath.

Next, an interview with Marlin Jones, charged with stalking and harassment after the funeral, now with additional charges added including kidnapping. He was currently at the Melbourne Remand Centre, the assessment prison not far from Melbourne Crime Command in the central business district.

I called Swanson.

"Jack. Where are you at?" She was in the car judging by the background noise. She had me on speakerphone.

"About to pay a visit to Marlin Jones at MRC."

"It'll take me an hour to get there."

Garrett turned and nodded at me. "It's okay, Ed Garrett will tag along," I said.

She pushed out a breath of air. "Yeah, all right. Let me know when the cell door slams shut."

"You'll be there. I'll let you know." I hung up and grabbed my jacket.

Garrett already had his wallet, and we walked down the corridor, out through the front door, and onto the street.

"Easy, Jack, eh?" He held the lift door open and I thanked him with a nod.

"Don't worry, I won't lay a finger on him. But he's mine. We're closing in and he knows it." Both of us took a moment, off in our own worlds, streaming various scenarios through our minds. Mentally, I prepared myself, closed my eyes for a second and slowed my breathing.

Outside, I pulled my jacket closer, and braced against the wind. The walk took us no longer than a couple of minutes.

We arrived at the MRC, said our greetings, showed our identifications and signed in. We then waited in the interview room for Marlin Jones to be brought in.

"I'll lead," I said to Garrett, who nodded, a pensive look on his face. His legs and arms were crossed. He sat on one side of the grey battered table, back against one wall, while I sat directly on the side of the table that faced the metal door.

I wanted to see Marlin's face when he walked in.

There were clunking noises as the door was unlocked. A dark-haired oak tree of a prison officer opened the door, entered the room and stood aside.

Marlin Jones was still thin, and paler than the last time I'd seen him. I caught a split second of recognition on his face, a look of horror and fear. But he recovered quickly and smiled. "Well, Jack Fletcher, what an unexpected surprise."

Garrett and I exchanged a look. I leaned back in the chair.

"Who's looking after the girls while you're inside Marlin? They didn't do much of a job."

Jones didn't flinch. Instead, he stared right through me, holding a fixed stare.

"There were seventeen young girls, I counted 'em." Garrett leaned forward in the chair, resting one hand on his right leg.

Marlin Jones threw his head back and laughed, long and loud. "Ah, you'll never find him. Never." He sat back in the seat and extended his legs in front of him and stared at his toes.

"I wouldn't be too sure of that, dick head." I wanted to reach over and grab him by the neck with both hands but suppressed the urge. I wouldn't stoop to the level of this sicko, no matter how much it hurt pushing down the desire to kill him with my bare hands.

"Oh, but I'm sure. We are on this side of the table, you're on that side, wearing prison gear. Your laptop was interesting reading, by the way." Said Garrett.

Marlin's smile dropped. I decided to push on, leaning further across the table.

"You have quite a few interested buyers, Jones. It would go a lot easier on you if you gave us his name. Then we could start talking for real." I said.

Jones pushed his lips together firmly and crossed his arms. Any trace of cockiness had long since vanished. *Fucker*.

"Shy, Marlin? According to the girls, you weren't shy." Heat prickled across my face.

"Didn't touch them."

"Yeah, right." Garrett raised his rump from the chair, thought better of it, then sat down again.

"Either way, we got him now that we have the laptop. Our techs are working on it as we speak. The question is, how far will you go to protect the son of a bitch?" I kept my voice calm, low, cool.

Marlin swallowed, the lump slowly making its way down his skinny grey throat. "He'll kill me, though."

Neither Garrett nor I spoke for a few seconds, mulling over our next move. While having Marlin Jones dead sounded appealing, maybe we could leverage Marlin's fear that the guy would find him and arrange for his death in jail.

"So, he knows people, huh? In that case, the more you tell us, the safer you are." I'd made one last attempt, then we were out of here. A look between Garrett and me confirmed my plan.

"Not telling you fuckers anything." Marlin looked at the floor.

"Roll out the red carpet. He'll be in here before you know it. Or his people will. You're on your own." I was done.

Garrett and I scraped back our chairs simultaneously. We were up and at the door in the blink of an eye. The prison guard began unlocking the various bars to open the door. Marlin didn't move. We were out of the door in a split second and striding down the corridor towards the security area, then out onto the street. My heart banged so hard I wondered if it would jump out of my chest.

My jacket pocket buzzed. Niki Newhouse was calling.

"What have you got for me, Niki?"

"Not the winning lotto tickets, unfortunately," she said.

I stopped, waiting for the blow.

"Although I do have an email you might be interested in."

Constricted throat. Can't breathe.

"Who?"

"Doesn't say, but judging by the history, looks like his name's Eric Slavosky."

Fucking bastard had been under my nose the whole time! I took a breath.

"Thanks Niki" I said and hung up.

Prickles raced along my shoulders, my back, my neck. A pounding filled my ears and my pulse ratcheted up into overdrive.

A picture of Gemma came to me, playing in the backyard with the prick, laughing and giggling as she threw the ball back to him... and then that slimy fucker's face, twisted in a smile of satisfaction.

I clenched my fists, remembered his curiosity at Crime Command, the questions about the job and if there were any leads.

I remembered my mother's advice, too: *Rise above it, son, rise above it.*

At the time, it had seemed strange, but now I knew what she meant. Don't stoop to the level of evil. Justice would be the best revenge, the slam of the gavel. All the same, I wanted to beat the fucker to a pulp.

"What? You got a name?" Garrett paused inches from my face, his smoker's breath overpowering.

"Boyfriend of the ex-wife. Eric Slavosky. The fucker. Hidden from view and convincing. I fell for it hook, line and fucking sinker." I shoved my phone back in my pocket and power-walked down the street back to Crime Command.

"Hang on, Jack!" Ed Garrett struggled to catch up and grabbed at my elbow. I shoved his hand away.

"Calm and cool, mate. Slow down."

Fuck, he had a point. I didn't look at him but slowed my pace to his and shoved both hands in the pockets of my pants.

"Need a hand with the arrest warrant?"

"That'd be great. Once I see Niki and check out the email for myself, we're all over him like a rash. I need to talk to Hicks too."

The lights changed to red and we stopped at the crossing at the back of a crowd of pedestrians. My mind was in overdrive. The concept of sleeping without drowning in grog loomed closer. "That's right, mate," said Garrett. "You got him, so close you can touch it. The peace of sleep is yours."

Fucking almost. I could taste the bitter tang of justice on my tongue.

Rae Swanson and I could celebrate tonight. This time, though, with lemonade.

When I got back to Crime Command, I went straight to Niki's desk. She had the laptop powered up and waiting.

"Here it is Jack. Email address slickandhandsome@gmail.com." I blew out a breath and shifted my weight from one hip to the other. "I tracked the email address and his IP and turns out he lives in Croydon. Here's the screenshot."

Eric Slavosky appeared on a white screen with green and blue text on the larger screen to the back left. Slick and fucking handsome. Not.

Niki pointed to the smaller screen of the laptop. "There's the original exchange."

My stomach curdled. Eric and Marlin, Scumbags Inc. Eric had arranged for the abduction and kidnap of Jessica, and in this case, Eric had arranged to keep the goods for himself as working capital.

Fuck.

"Thanks, Niki." I walked off.

"Go get 'em, Jack." Niki's voice trailed behind me. I got to my desk, and Garrett spun around triumphantly.

"Got it, mate. Arrest warrant. I've emailed it to the Magistrates Court. It's still business hours so we should have it urgently."

"Thanks, I'll give them a call."

"Already done. We should have an answer soon, especially for Project Beacon; it's all over the airwaves." He looked down at his phone which didn't ring.

But mine did.

I picked it up almost before it rang.

"DS Fletcher?"

"Yes." My pulse quickened for the second time that day.

"You have your warrant. I'm faxing it through to Crime Command now."

"Thank you. You have the number?" she read it back to me.

I hung up and smiled at Garrett, then jumped up for an air punch. "We got him, Ed. We fucking got him."

Garrett high-fived me, never a hugger, thank God. "Let's take a trip to Croydon."

"Let me call Hicks, then Swanson."

"No problem, I'll alert the whole team."

CHAPTER TWENTY-TWO

I BRACED MYSELF FOR the cold, pulling my jacket tighter as I walked down the path to the front door of Melinda Holmes and Eric Slavosky. Garrett and Swanson followed behind me and quickened their steps to catch up. Garrett shot me pensive looks, hands shoved in his jeans pockets.

Melinda Holmes had the door open before we arrived. She stood arms crossed, weight hanging over one hip.

"Don't tell me, you've actually done your job?"

Swanson stared at me, but I didn't look at her. I kept my eyes on the mother.

"May we come in?"

"I guess," Melinda Holmes stood back to allow us entry, closing the door firmly behind us.

The worm was sipping on a glass of water when we entered the living area.

I pulled the cuffs from the back of my pocket and he put the glass down on the coffee table and backed away. I grabbed his right hand and spun him around. "Eric Slavosky, you're under arrest for the rape and murder of Jessica Holmes."

"Fuck off!," he screamed, and I bent him over the back of the couch and growled in his ear "She was seven years old you piece of fucking shit."

Rae began to speak, but lunged for Melinda Holmes who screamed profanities, shrieking and howling like a fishwife. But then, she had just learned that the man she'd been sleeping with had raped and killed her daughter.

"Is this true, you fucking arsehole? Is it?"

Eric backed away from her, but Melinda Holmes was gunning for him.

In a split-second Melinda was out of the living area, down the hall and banging around in the kitchen. Rae Swanson strode after her, as did I, and she flicked a look at me.

Melinda's face was mottled red, eyes bulging and mouth open. She lifted her right hand, the large kitchen knife blade extending from the bottom of her hand. Tiny drops of blood dripped from her hand where she'd grabbed at the handle, most likely in a mad hurry, and cut herself.

"Die, you bastard die!" She rushed back to the living area and lunged for Eric, throwing herself across the table. Swanson grabbed her from behind, me from the front. She collapsed onto the ground sobbing, huge racking sobs, where she could barely catch her breath. Swanson rubbed Melinda's back as she did so.

My soul shattered into a million pieces, a soul I thought I'd lost a piece of forever, that had blackened and charred. Will Holmes, Melinda Holmes, the young girls, their families, my family. All because of Eric Slavosky's sick and twisted need to consume and possess young girls.

I walked away from Melinda towards Eric. He'd quietened down now, but he didn't attempt to apologise, or beg forgiveness.

I lifted him up by his handcuffed arms.

He turned to face me, unmoving, still and silent. "You've got a nerve coming in here and arresting me, ruining my family. Where's your evidence?"

Without breaking the stare, I handed Slavosky off to Garrett, and removed a thin rubber glove from my pocket. I picked up the glass from the table, and lifted it in a cheers gesture, to Eric Slavosky.

"Right here," I said, and brought a plastic bag from my other pocket, placing the glass inside and sealing it with the Ziplock. I allowed myself a rare smile, savouring the warmth that filled my chest.

Eric's face paled, the blood suddenly draining out of it and sinking to his shoes.

"Don't be too sure of yourself," I said. Rae now sat at the table and had caught her breath. Melinda was at her side, drinking a glass of water. A box of tissues beside in front of her, she continued to wipe at her face. She didn't look at me or Eric, she probably couldn't. Rae whispered to Melinda, and with the tilt of her chin, left the room via the rear entrance. Rae seemed to be good at soothing frayed nerves and putting people at ease.

A woman's touch maybe. She could certainly teach me a few things.

I grabbed at Eric's handcuffs pulling them tighter and he screamed. I didn't bother apologising.

I increased pressure.

"This is police brutality, I know my rights. I'm going to sue you and the whole department." The pitch had changed, higher more unstable, almost shrill.

"Go for your life. Trust me, I'm controlling myself. I haven't hurt you. Not sure if I can say the same for the boys inside, they're really friendly I hear." I allowed myself another smile.

I stood hard up behind him as he didn't want to go anywhere. I didn't want to leave Rae behind but as a seasoned detective, she'd look after Melinda Holmes.

Eric had stopped, so I pushed him by the elbows.

I grabbed at his left elbow, and Garrett shoved at Slavosky's right. Between us we got him out the door and down the footpath.

Once we arrived at the car, Garrett decided to speak "Get in arsehole." I recognised that stone voice, a point where seething anger had shifted to the calmest warning he could manage.

Slavosky glared at both of us, so Garrett pushed him in by the head.

"Ow! Fuck you."

I slammed the door shut and stared across the top of the car at Garrett who had moved across to the driver's side. I got in.

This would be interesting. Obviously, both of us wanted to the kill the guy, who wouldn't?

But we had to play this by the book, part of the fun of being a representative of law-abiding citizens. Showing leadership and setting a good example and all that.

Maybe now I could be a real example to my wife and kids, throw away the bottle and be a human being again.

Live life, or at least half a life.

As Garrett started the car, I thought about Maddy, her bright shining face, pushing happiness out at the world, eyes shining.

I looked around at the shit bag in the back seat. Pale face, he stared out through the window, head turned to the left.

The day had turned damp and gray, and the trees hung their heads in shame.

The image of my daughter wouldn't leave. An image of some creep grabbing her from a park, bundling her into a car.

I shivered.

"Where are we going? I need to make a phone call. It's my right." Slavosky sounded indignant, annoyed.

Garrett and I ignored him for a moment, then I spoke, without turning back to look at him. I bit back the response I wanted to give and kept it cool. Anything else would give my temper free reign, and that was a loose cannon to nowhere.

"Jessica doesn't have rights anymore. That was her name, Jessica. Her father lost his rights too, the right to hold his daughter."

The worm was wising up. He didn't speak again.

We took Footscray Road to the M1 freeway, heading for the King Street exit through the central business district. Traffic was light at this time of the morning, all the business people in their offices, slaving away at cubicles, enduring a different kind of hell to mine. My hell involved suppressing the desire to harm Eric Slavosky.

"You'll need to be searched and processed," Garrett said, keeping his voice quiet. If there was one thing that scared people, it was Ed Garrett when he went quiet. Yelling was the easy part.

"Who'll do that? You?" I stretched my neck around to see Eric's wide, terrified eyes. I smiled and turned back to stare straight ahead.

"You never know your luck in a big city." Garrett peered into the rear view mirror and smiled.

Slavosky began kicking the front seats, so hard that Garrett's headrest jolted forward. Without missing a beat, Garrett flicked on the indicator and the flashing lights and pulled over into the King Street bus lane.

"Stay in the car, Ed," I said. But Ed Garrett was out and barely looked back at me. I opened my door to stand on the left-hand passenger side, closer to a concrete barrier, where construction works were going on. Garrett jerked on the door handle and swung the door open. Slavosky reared backwards on the back seat.

"Easy, Ed," I said, out of earshot. At least, so I hoped.

"Fuck off, Jack." Garrett was out of breath, leaning into the car. I pulled Garrett back by his belt, and he staggered backwards. I shoved the car door closed with my left knee.

"What the fuck are you doing? That piece of shit has it coming." Veins pulsed in Garrett's forehead.

"Stopping you from fucking this case up. I'm not going back to the bottle." I shoved my hands in my jeans pockets to stop me waving them around. Slavosky's face was pressed up against the window. He'd now begun kicking the inside of the doors. I put one arm around Garrett's shoulders and steered him away from the car, towards the barrier and the trees beyond.

Garrett pushed out a breath. "I'm not a dickhead, Jack, I know how it rolls, but I just want one minute, one minute with the fucker."

I paused, thinking about what to say next. "Well I am a dickhead. I haven't seen my kids since Abbie moved in with her sister, and I've gone through so many bottles of Johnny Walker, I need a new bin to hold the empties."

Garrett walked off a few steps, staring at the trees. He dropped his head, then walked back. The red mottled veins on veins on his face had stopped throbbing.

"I'm sorry, mate."

"Don't be sorry, Ed. Let's get this fucker. We have to play it by the book."

"No one will know."

"We'll know."

Ed Garrett swore under his breath. "Yeah, okay."

"Don't look at him or talk to him. He's cuffed, we can get another car. But we won't get another chance to lock him up. For good."

A glazed curtain closed over Garrett's eyes, and the muscles in his jaw relaxed. He offered a tight nod. Garrett walked around the car and got into the driver's side.

I swung the front passenger door open and then closed it quietly. Slavosky recommenced the swearing, the screaming, the kicking.

Collen turned the radio up full volume. He flicked on the right indicator, and finding a gap, hit the accelerator and swung the car back onto the freeway.

We took the King Street freeway exit. As we slowed down, Slavosky's screams subsided, and he muttered and sighed.

I slid my mobile phone from the inside pocket of my jacket and rang ahead to the remand centre or MAP.

"Hello, MAP." Melbourne Assessment Prison, sometimes also referred to as Melbourne Remand Centre held inmates until sentenced.

"Hi. DS Fletcher, Crime Command. On the way with male early forties, alleged child serial killer, pending charges of stalking and kidnap. Sexual Offences Unit most likely."

"Right. Bring him in, we'll take care of him."

"Thanks, Doug," I hung up. Doug, late fifties, had been around longer than I had.

"Fuck you bastards," Slavosky piped up, testing his vocal cords. Both Garrett and I barely blinked. We drove into the sloped drive of the MAP.

Heat surged through my chest. We pulled up and I opened the glove box. The glass, contained within its plastic bag insulation, glared at me, reminding me it shouldn't be there, but in the lab.

Garrett stopped the car and put it in park. His face was a mask, a layer of glass that had fallen. We got out of the car. I walked around and stood next to him as he opened the back passenger door.

"Get out." Although to most people he may have sounded quiet and commanding, I recognised the barbed wire in his voice.

Slavosky complied and got out, looked at both of us, then spat on the floor. Garrett yanked him by the handcuffs and Eric squealed.

We walked to the main reception, where Eric would be processed. He'd be stripped, showered and searched. Shame neither of us would be around for that.

We walked through to the desk, dragging the worm with us, and handed the paperwork over that I'd filled out in the car.

The white counter had flaked in places, and the white plastic had lifted, leaving tiny black holes in random positions.

A short dark-haired man with a name tag that read 'John Hall' accepted the paperwork, which he held in both hands close to his face. He stared at the papers and then looked up.

"We'll take it from here."

I handed my card over. "If you need it."

John gave me a knowing look. "Right."

Garrett stood as still as a statue; previously, he'd shifted his weight ever so slightly from one foot to the other, barely noticeable to others, but a neon sign to me. Slavosky was taken away and moved out of sight at the end of the corridor. Collen sighed and rubbed at his forehead.

"Let's get this glass to the lab," I said to Garrett, but he didn't move or register that I'd spoken. I understood how he felt without a doubt, but progress on the case had lifted the dark cloud from my shoulders, so I pressed on. It was the only thing keeping me in the present. The thought of Slavosky sentenced, and behind bars for life, away from any other children.

Eventually, Garrett turned and joined me in the walk back to the car park, his boots clacking on the linoleum, taking precise steps.

The drive back to Melbourne Crime Command was subdued, but calm. I wondered if this would be the end of it. Based on experience, most likely not. Eric Slavosky would probably drag this out for as long as he could, judging by his violent protests about his innocence.

But then, paedophilic serial killers could surprise the best cops in all sorts of sick ways.

CHAPTER TWENTY-THREE

AFTER VISITING THE lab and dropping the glass off, I paced for a while, then went through all the information I'd accumulated since the start of the job.

It was still light at lunchtime, although the sky had darkened in places, with a storm threatening to break through. I stayed focussed on the task, poring over every report, each syllable burning into my brain.

Garrett, Wallace and I had split the file into sections.

Swanson arrived not long after and swung a free-standing chair around, firmly establishing herself to the left of us.

"Can I help?" she extended a hand.

"Is that a question?"

"No." She smiled as I handed over a section of paperwork.

My phone buzzed. Selena Hicks. A text.

Meeting in briefing room. Now. Project Beacon.

"Okay folks, boss lady wants a pow-wow."

Swanson stood up immediately, adjusting her jacket over curves I'd done my best not to notice and walked away.

Wallace and Garrett weren't far behind.

As I headed down the corridor, I saw a couple of other detectives striding from the opposite end of the corridor.

Hicks didn't want to mess around today. The board was still up, including photos of Jessica Holmes, Baker, Taylor Wentworth, Bianca Baker and Louisa Fein, one of Swanson's earlier child murder cases.

Eric Slavosky, the scumbag's picture, and those of the rescued girls were underneath those along with one of Marlin Jones.

After we'd all circulated and gathered to stand inside the door and around the walls, Hicks' voice rang out, clear and true.

"Okay, who's coordinating evidence?"

"I've been through the Fein case and compared it to the Holmes job. Almost identical except for the method of murder." Swanson volunteered this information first.

"And?" Hicks' feathers barely ruffled.

"I've been in touch with DS Fletcher and SoCIT."

"Great. Tighten it up, I want this a formality. Let's put Slavosky away. Do we have a confession?"

"Not yet." I figured I'd better speak up considering all my thoughts had been consumed by the job.

"When?"

"I'll go down after the meeting."

"Great. Holmberg, Wallace, find out the status of the rescued girls, and talk to Jones again, connect Slavosky to the house where the girls were kept. Davis, Harris, we might need to cut a deal with Jones to get him to talk. Let me know."

Davis and Harris must have been from the police prosecutor's office.

They nodded. Feet shuffled, and throats were cleared, with a couple of muffled comments.

"Before you go. Good work everyone. I know this has been a tough case for all of us, but you've stayed the course. Now, let's go get our reward."

I walked out towards the car park. I'd sent a text to Will Holmes earlier, but no reply. I'd go see him after the interview with Slavosky.

Reaching the car park, I pressed the unlock button, I got into my car, and thought about my daughters. Abbie had called the night before to set up a meeting, due to take place this Sunday.

Hopefully, I'd need no more than a nightcap to send me off to the land of nod, all being well. It all rode on the confession. I'd need to change tactics, play his game, understand him, offer some compassion. That was never something I enjoyed; I knew I could do it though, if need be, even if I wanted to hurt him, badly.

I drove rather than walking, parked the car, and headed into the main entrance. I walked down the white tiled corridor towards the main desk for the cells, pulling out my ID as I walked. I stopped at the desk, wide, with a series of other desks behind it.

Dave was still there.

"Back to see your mate?"

"Something like that."

I signed the register Dave shoved my way.

"Go on through." The buzzer blared, and I pulled the heavy door open as the lock clicked. I walked down the long corridor, calm washing over me. I'd done as my long-suffering mother had advised; I'd risen above it, for a purpose, to put the worm away for a long time, I hoped.

Hands in pockets, I reached the makeshift meeting room at the end of the corridor on the right.

I sat back and surveyed the room. A metal table was nailed to the floor.

Paint was peeling off the walls—or had been ripped off. I stretched my shoulders.

Another buzzer sounded, and I heard the clanging of locks from the door on my right.

In came the skinny runt with head held high, hands cuffed. The officer stood between us at the right-hand side of the table and Slavosky sat, extending out his legs. He smiled up at the burly dark-haired officer, a fellow bearded gent.

Mr. Beard didn't smile back.

The officer nodded at me. "I won't be far away."

"Thanks."

He pushed a button, the buzzer sounding off again and the door clanging shut. The sound reverberated throughout the small bare room.

"What the fuck do you want?"

"A chat." I pulled a recorder out of my pocket, hit the record button and laid it on the table. "I'm going to record our chat, okay?"

"I don't like the way you chat."

"How about a DNA test?"

"No way."

I figured as much, but confidence had descended. He was within reach, and the end to my alcoholic binges was near, and I had news to give to Will Holmes. It wouldn't bring his daughter back, but it would bring an end, maybe a resolution somehow.

"It doesn't matter, we have the glass. The lab has it now."

The fucking worm paled, much to my satisfaction. He pressed his lips together and shuffled in his seat. I needed to press further, but in the right way. Interviewing suspects was always a gamble; they could be pushed, but not too far. They could be prodded, questioned, while a team behind the scenes got the evidence to push further. It was an intense need to put the dregs of society away, mitigated by the law.

There was only one way to get him, a strategy I hadn't tried yet.

Good cop, understanding cop, helpful cop.

I got up from the nailed-down seat and grabbed a wooden chair from the side of the room. It scraped across the chipped linoleum floor and I dragged it next to Slavosky.

"All those bad feelings you have, the sadness, the loneliness; it will go away if you do the right thing."

"Bullshit." Slavosky turned his head away towards the door, which contained a small secure reinforced window. Burly Beard brought his head close to the glass.

"I've been there. I've made mistakes. Big mistakes. It's hard being a man, the pressure, the loneliness, it adds up."

Slavosky didn't answer. He lowered his head.

"If you do the right thing, come clean, the bad feeling will go away. I know how you feel, I've been there."

Slavosky raised his head and rubbed one skinny hairy hand across his mouth. I watched him carefully for a sign, any indication of where this was going.

His eyes reddened.

I waited. After an eternity that was probably more like thirty seconds, he moved his hand away. He sighed.

"So, if I tell you, what happens?"

"You'll feel better. Straight away. You can sleep at night, the bad feeling inside, the loneliness will go. I promise."

His mouth quivered, and he paused to compose himself. Then he spoke in a monotone. "The first one, she died too quickly. Then I met Jessica, beautiful Jessica."

My body tensed, and heat flushed through my body. "Go on, tell me all of it. Get it all out. It will help."

"The first girl had dark hair, the daughter of my ex-girl-friend. We lived together, she was..." Slavosky paused, staring off into space. "So beautiful, so pure. So, I asked my friend to take her somewhere special, somewhere secret."

"Marlin Jones."

Slavosky turned to look out of the only excuse for a window again. He sighed and turned back but couldn't look at me. Instead, he stared at the far wall.

"Yes. He kept them in the house until I was ready."

My stomach curdled.

"You're doing great, keep going. You need to tell the truth, let it out, you'll feel better after you tell the truth."

"I guess. I'm still not sure."

"You're already partway there. Keep going with me here, get it all out. It's the only way."

"I met Melinda at the school, after parent-teacher inter-views one night. Louisa was already gone. Mel showed me pho-tos of her daughters, Jessica got my attention straight away. I took my time, getting to know Mel, Gemma and Jessica." Slavosky paused, smiling briefly, staring at the ground, then raising his head and sighing.

"How did you kill her?"

"The first girl, Louisa, she went so quickly. So, with Jessica, I went back to the group home, took my time."

I swallowed hard and shifted my chair closer.

"How did you kill her?"

Slavosky looked up as if for some divine inspiration. God might forgive him, but no way in hell would I.

"I put my hands around her neck until she passed out. She was out so long, I figured she'd died, so I tried out my CPR. It worked."

I couldn't speak. After an interminable few seconds, he spoke again.

"She came back to life. So, I tied her up, hung her up, and this time it was slower. Tiny cuts, lots of tiny cuts and burns. She cried out at first, then she stopped."

My arms ached, and my throat burned. "Where are her clothes?"

"They're at my place, her underwear and clothes, under the house in the crawl space, in her backpack."

I picked up the recorder and turned it off. I pushed my chair back and walked towards the door, knocking on the window. The sick feeling had grown.

"Where are you going? I'm not finished."

I gritted my teeth and spoke without looking at him. "You're going away for a long time. For the rest of your sick fucking life. Where you belong."

Eric stood up. "But you said I'd feel better."

I knocked on the window. I'd heard enough, didn't want to see the piece of shit again. I needed a shower, to wash the crawling slime off my skin. "Officer!"

Burly Beard arrived and opened the door.

I wanted to run down the corridor. Instead, I walked quickly, hoping my skin would stop crawling the farther away I got from Eric Slavosky, evil incarnate.

The guard pushed the button to open the next screening door. Through the window encased in mesh, stood Selena Hicks.

All I saw were her eyes, wide as saucers.

"Thanks," I said to the guard, who nodded in reply.

I took a few steps towards boss lady, who leaned back against the wall. She looked drawn and pale.

"What's going on?," I tried to keep it low key, a pressure valve, but the both of us knew something shitty had happened.

"You got the confession?"

"Yeah."

"Well that's something, well done. Now we have another problem. Will Holmes just found out Eric Slavosky was the one that tortured, raped and killed his daughter."

"Holy shit," I kept my voice low. Although the guards had retreated behind the desk, I figured they'd heard more than they let on. "Let's walk."

Selena walked towards the hallway and hung a right towards the lifts. The hallway was empty. She shoved her hands in her pockets.

"Neighbour called, hearing the screams. Will had gone over to her place and pulled a knife on her."

I wasn't sure if I'd heard her properly. I was careful to keep my tone controlled. "Did you say Will tried to kill his ex?"

She pulled her hands out of her pockets, putting them up in a gesture of surrender, but it was more likely an attempt to calm me down.

"Officers are there. I thought you should know."

I swore under my breath. Obviously, there were hidden depths to Will Holmes. I hadn't picked up on the seething anger, tentacles unfurling.

A tall thin guy with glasses walked by, casting a stare in our direction.

Boss lady pointed her eyebrows towards the exit. I started walking.

Out on the street, the noise was deafening. Pedestrian crossing controls clicked and beeped, horns honked, and business people laughed and chatted.

I stopped at the curb, a couple of metres down from the intersection. The pedestrian crossing clicker quietened down obediently.

I pulled out my phone and stared at it. "Garrett and Wallace are there?"

"Yeah. You know this guy, Jack, you're a father. I figured you could talk him down from the ledge."

"Thanks." I wondered if I could. I'd spent the last couple of weeks in an alcoholic daze that I'd only emerged from the last few days. Was I up to it?

Reading my thoughts, Selena Hicks pressed the point. "You got a confession, Jack. That's something."

I looked back at her. Her eyes glinted in the sun.

"I gotta go. I'll call the guys on the way."

I should have listened when Will Holmes told me he'd kill the guy that did this. He couldn't get to Slavosky, so he'd chosen the next best thing.

His ex-wife.

I had to get to the car park and drive over to Slavosky's place, before Will killed two birds with one stone.

CHAPTER TWENTY-FOUR

THE SKY WAS A RIBBON of clear blue. I thought about Will Holmes. I wasn't a religious guy in any way, shape or form, but at that moment, I offered up a silent prayer.

God, if you stop Will Holmes before he hurts Melinda, I'll consider coming back. Seriously.

I got into my car, an unmarked Ford Falcon sedan. The quiet warmth didn't do much to combat the nausea and adrenaline invading my system.

"Call Ed Garrett," I called out to no one in particular. The familiar tones of the car's equivalent of Siri told me she was calling him.

"Ed, what's the go?" The guy was still in the house by the sound of it, although I didn't hear screams.

"We're en route. He's in his car. He didn't kill his ex, he threatened her and took off, but came pretty close. A female officer got to their place, just after Will left, they're with Melinda Holmes now"

Shit.

I tried to swallow, but a lump the size of a house brick prevented it. My temperature was up. I gripped the steering wheel tighter.

"Where?"

"In Kew, he's heading for the freeway, Chandler Highway entrance, I'd say."

"I'm leaving the city now. What's he driving?"

"Black XR6 turbo. Reg WIL399"

"Thanks." I hung up.

Distinctive. I pulled out of the car park and flicked the switch. The indicators flashed, and the siren squawked.

Dickheads wouldn't move out of the way at the intersection as per usual. I swerved to miss a white van that sprung out of Latrobe street to my right.

I saw the sign announcing the entrance to the freeway and swung into the left lane. The entrance was about 800 metres left. Thankfully, at around 11am, traffic was light.

Anguish burned through my veins. I'd put myself in harm's way if I had to. Thinking about Will Holmes, I had some idea of what he was going through, although I didn't pretend I'd ever fully understand; losing a child to the worst kind of murder was every father's nightmare. Will had lost his daughter in the most horrific ways, memories most likely etched into his brain forever.

Losing one of my girls in that way was something I couldn't think of; I'd already seen too much. The hairs on the back of my neck were up, along with those on my arms.

I turned left over a bridge and was on the freeway. The truck in front of me didn't move, so I veered into the fast lane where a red Ute swerved left, then right. I leaned my hand heavily on the horn, which blared loudly. I changed lanes, back into the middle.

My chest burned, and my head buzzed. The two-way radio sparked into life.

"Armed suspect outbound on M3. Three vehicles in pursuit."

Maybe rather than a knife, Will Holmes had somehow got hold of a gun. He'd kept that quiet but then the father of a murdered daughter hellbent on revenge didn't exactly announce his intentions to the world.

I swung into the lane for the M3, and hit the horn, again. A silver Holden Barina moved away from the exit.

I revved the shit out of the Ford Falcon and saw Garrett's car in the middle lane. He was probably doing at least 130 kilometres an hour. I floored it to try match him, my chest drumming a heavy metal tune.

I took the right lane, no concept of failure or sudden death. I had to get to Will before he killed himself or other drivers, and time was running out.

I focussed on the road, awareness heightened and a combination of fear and determination buzzing through my veins.

"Suspect ahead; we need to block the Bourke Road exit."

I gunned it, hoping my car was up to the task. Garrett was about two hundred metres ahead.

"Suspect is heading for the exit."

I saw the flashing lights, and the tyre spikes ahead on the left. I switched lanes, narrowly missing a green corolla. It was time to end this.

Will's car ran over the spikes, then crashed into the fluorescent orange and white barriers, the right quarter panel of the car spinning first. Then the XR6 turbo squealed to a stop. I pulled up in the emergency lane on his left. Garrett and Wallace were already out of the car, along with several uniforms.

All weapons pointed at the car. For a long minute, nothing happened other than yelling.

"Get out of the car! Show your weapon!" No response.

I had to judge the right time to get across to Will. Another fluoro barrier had been set up and traffic sped past at high speeds. I picked my way across the road, around officers with their weapons drawn, flashed my badge and made it to the side of the car. I stood beside Garrett. He didn't react, gun drawn and pointed at the driver's door which opened a few centimeters. No weapon.

"Drop your weapon, now!" Garrett's voice was loud and angry as hell.

I crept forward, slowly edging closer to the driver's side door of Will's car. Open just a centimeter or two, I pried it open slightly. Will sat back in the seat, dazed, eyes barely open, a gun on his lap. He did have a knife, but at that point, he'd laid it on the passenger seat. Angry purple weals, possibly scratches, marked his right cheek.

"Back away, Jack." I ignored Ed Garrett calling from behind. I nudged the door open even further with my right knee and squatted down, inches away from Will.

I didn't believe Will would hurt me. Sure, he'd committed a crime, and I wasn't condoning that. But as a Father, I thought I understood him. Although I'd never voice it, I wondered how I'd react if a scumbag like Slavosky raped, tortured and killed my baby girl. Would I try to kill him, or if I couldn't kill him, try to kill the next best thing, the ex-wife who'd brought the piece of shit into their lives?

I had no answer.

I did feel a wave of compassion for the guy.

"Will," I said quietly. No response. His eyes were still glazed and staring off into the distance. "Will, are you okay?" I shifted a little closer. He turned his face towards me. His eyes flickered briefly, as he registered me there. Then tears ran down his face and his expression crumpled.

"Fuck. Jessica. What have I done, my girl?" Will covered his face with both hands.

My chest felt like someone had wrung it out, an old dish-cloth. "I'm here to help, Will."

I turned to see Garrett had attempted to move closer, but with a barely perceptible signal, my nod to him, he backed away. I held up five fingers behind my back. Five minutes. Just give me five fucking minutes.

"It's too late. I should have kept my girl safe. Jessica, I'm coming." In the blink of an eye, Will had the weapon up and pointed it as his temple.

Goosebumps rose on my legs, my back. Fuck. I understood. Staring off into the distance, I realised he wanted to be with Jessica. "Mate, it's not where you want to be. Gemma needs you, she wants her Dad here with her."

"Bullshit. I just tried to kill her bitch of a mother, how do I tell her that?"

I had no idea where the words came from, but they came. "Tell her the truth. Kids understand more than we know. She can take it, and so can you."

Will hung his head and sobbed harder. He didn't drop the gun, still holding it at his temple.

I waited. Hoping like hell he wouldn't do the unthinkable. I fixed my gaze on his finger, held over the trigger. Thankfully, at that moment, his finger hadn't connected with it. Behind us, traffic sped, and cops waited with guns drawn. I looked back at Collen and extended a flat hand, bringing it down. He dropped his chin and his weapon, signalling behind him for officers to do the same.

"Why? I trusted her, and that fucking parasite of a boyfriend... and he—" He collapsed into grief again. I extended an open palm to him.

"Take my hand, Will."

I lifted his head to meet my gaze. His eyes were filled, tears running down his nose. He had a cut on his eyes and his mouth contorted. "I can't do this anymore, man. Do you understand? I can't fucking do it,"

"I do understand. But you can, and you will. Gemma needs you, Jessica needs you. She wouldn't want you to do this," Will wiped his face with his left sleeve. He still had the gun at his temple but had lowered it now to his jaw.

"We need you at the court case. Look evil in the eye and show him you're a survivor."

"I don't know if I can."

"You can. Think about Gemma. I'm a father, I have daughters nearly the same age as yours."

Will stared at me, pain radiating out from him so deeply it almost hummed. He didn't speak so I continued.

"Gemma loves you like no one else can. Like only a little girl can love her daddy. Don't take that from her. She needs you."

Will lowered the weapon, dropping it onto his lap. I extended my right hand out to him, leaving it hovering. "Give me the gun, Will."

With lips trembling, he handed it over. I took the weapon and stood up, extending my left hand to him. "Give yourself up, Will. It will be rough, I'm not going to pretend this will all go away, but you can face it. You're stronger than you think."

He placed his hand in mine. "Well done, Will. You got this. I'm going to call for an ambulance to check you over okay? Then you'll be charged."

Will didn't answer.

Garrett walked over, took the weapon and after helping Will up, I walked away. Away from Garrett, away from the officers, further down past the ambulance, where Will was being escorted.

I needed a minute to decompress. I stopped underneath a bridge about a hundred metres away.

Will would probably be charged with attempted murder, but all being well, he'd get a suspended sentence. Fathers of raped, tortured and murdered seven-year-old girls generally met with sympathy from juries. So much destruction and devastation.

Garrett appeared, a serious look on his face. "Ambos are with him now."

"What a fucking mess."

"Yeah."

Garrett shoved his hands in his pockets, thought better of it, then removed them.

"You did good, Jack." He clapped me on the back.

"Maybe. But we've still got a dead little girl, and a father charged with attempted murder."

"Still can't take a fucking compliment, eh?"

I managed a grin. "Something like that."

"Take the rest of the day off."

"Yeah right. Until the next job. Fucking hell."

We both walked back around the concrete pillars, down the emergency lane towards the exit ramp. The tow truck winch lifted up the back end of Will's car, scrunched up accordion-like in the front where it had hit the barriers.

Will had gone, presumably in the back of the ambulance further down, and officers were now clumped together in groups, some with notepads in hands, others wiping the sweat out of their hair.

I stood in the middle of all of it, lost and adrift. I still had the recorder with Slavosky's confession, in my pocket. I had to drive it back to Crime Command.

I'd do that, then all I wanted was to see my daughters, hold them, kiss their hair, tell them I loved them.

CHAPTER TWENTY-FIVE

A SATURDAY MORNING looked different without a hang-over. I skipped the painkillers, and the bottles had long been relegated to the recycling bin. Today was the day I got to see my girls, Maddy and Molly, along with Abbie, A happy day, if such a thing was possible.

I'd actually taken today off, after Selena insisted. I'd even cleaned the place up, *shock, horror*. I'd opened up the doors and windows to air the place out when Abbie rang. I couldn't an-swer the phone quick enough, all fingers and thumbs when her name had appeared on my phone.

"Abbie?" I stretched my back, arching it, supported by my left hand at the base of my spine.

"Jack." Was that a smile I detected in her voice? Best not to get my hopes up, but I knew this woman.

"How about tomorrow? At Rosa's. Say, eleven?" Now she really was smiling. The girls murmured in the background.

I took a breath. "That would be.... great."

"Okay, see you then."

"Hang on, Abbie. Thanks, yeah?"

"You did have something to do with them being here, Jack. You're their father. It's okay. We'll see you tomorrow,"

She hung up. After the initial buzz of excitement, I'd finished my new-found interest in cleaning and watched a movie. The hours dragged. I consoled myself in the knowledge that should Abbie and the girls come back home, there'd be no complaints about the state of the house.

I might even win myself some brownie points; a few million would come in handy. I had backlogs.

Sunday morning, I'd sat in the car, parked outside Rosa's, with the radio playing quietly. The job was almost done. The case against Slavosky appeared watertight, but snakes could wiggle their way in or out of anything.

Will had been charged, and released on bail, although apparently, Melinda Holmes had taken out an intervention order to keep him away, with good reason.

My phone said 10.55 a.m., time to go inside. I got out of the car, locked it, and walked across the asphalt car park, dodging potholes. I couldn't see Abbie's car. Rosa's place looked to be moderately busy, the car park half full. An old shingle roof and aged brick with bay windows gave Rosa's a homely feel. It had been a second home for us for years, our go-to restaurant—back in the early days when I'd had time to spend with family, that is.

I pulled open the glass entry door. Warmth from the open fire wafted over me, combined with smells of garlic and red wine. I saw the girls straight away, standing beside the red vinyl seats of a corner booth just near the main entrance. Abbie smiled, her eyes moving from our daughters, to me. The girls smiled and looked around the room. It took a couple of seconds before they saw me.

I swallowed. Their beautiful faces, their delight at seeing me, struck me and I couldn't speak. Tears threatened to spill over the burning rims of my eyes.

Maddy broke into a run, dodging and weaving around tables. As she passed the register, she did a turn towards me, still in the vestibule area. Molly walked behind her, a smile on her face, allowing herself to look in my direction.

I squatted down and opened my arms. Maddy hugged me tightly first, wrapping her arms around my neck for a long moment. This time, I let the tears fall.

There was no one else here, just my girls, Maddy, Molly, and me. Maddy pulled away and Molly took a couple of steps forward. She paused.

I stood up. "I missed you, Dad." I brushed down her beautiful honey blonde hair. I'd almost forgotten what Molly's voice sounded like, pure and high pitched.

"I missed you too, but now I'm here. It's so good to see you, both of you." Taking a hesitant step, I smiled at Molly, unsure. She took three more steps into my arms. I hugged her, and after a second, she hugged me back, then let go. I held her by the shoulders. "Let's go eat and sit with Mum."

"Yeah!" Maddy jumped up, fist pumping above the half wall separating the lobby from the rest of the restaurant. I weaved my way through patrons and strode along the walkway which ran along the servery. Rosa, the manager, smiled at me.

Abbie looked good, the happiest I'd seen in a while. She'd let her blonde hair out for a change, not a ponytail in sight. Her cheeks were pink. She wore make up, and even better, I actually noticed she was wearing it. The girls slid across the red vinyl booth seats. Abbie stayed standing. "Hi." She looked at me, then looked away.

"It's good to see you."

"Yeah, well, the girls need you."

I need you, Abbie. I decided some things were better left unsaid. One step at a time as Abbie had reminded me a few days ago.

Abbie took a deep breath and rubbed her hands down the back of her jeans. "Right, let's order, shall we?" She took a seat at the end of the vinyl booth seats, and I sat directly opposite her.

"Yeah, I'm starving."

Maddy beamed at me. Abbie shot her a look.

I picked up a menu, doing my best to read it. I decided on the steak in a millisecond. Maddy gave Abbie her order then ran off to the gumball machine.

"Not too far, okay?" Abbie watched as she ran to the other side of the restaurant, at the end of the servery on the left. There was a children's play centre to the side of the gumball machine.

Molly shifted on her seat. "So, how's work, Dad?"

I took a minute to digest the question. How was work?

My little girl was growing up.

"It's better. We got the bad guy. I took yesterday off. Can you believe it?"

Abbie and Molly looked at me round-eyed. "Huh?" Molly rubbed her eyes.

"Don't worry, I might have surprised myself as well."

Abbie smiled.

"Let me know when the food comes, Mum, okay? I'll go check on Maddy."

"Thanks." Abbie stroked Molly's hair. "Come back soon, okay?"

"Okay, Mum." Abbie shifted across to let Molly out of the booth.

Abbie slid back in and clasped her hands together. A waitress came, exchanged pleasantries and took our orders.

"Soft drink? That's a nice change."

"Yeah, it is."

Outside, a lone grey cloud hung among blue sky. The car park began to fill up as the clock ticked closer to noon. I sat back and waited for whatever Abbie had to say.

"You fixed it, huh? Caught the bad guy?" Abbie tucked a lock of golden hair behind her ear, revealing a silver earring, which reflected the sunlight streaming in through the window.

"Yeah."

"That's good. How are you doing, Jack?"

"I'm getting there. Better, I guess,"

"Really?"

"Yeah, really. I filled up a bin with empties, haven't had a drink since last Wednesday."

"Wow."

"I even cleaned the place a bit."

"Now you're telling porky pies."

I laughed. "I miss you. All of you."

Abbie stared out the window, her eyes misted over. "I've learned to live without you," she said.

Stunned, I didn't reply.

"Not since I moved out, Jack. Well before that. I'm not saying it's over, but I promised myself I'd be honest with you. It's the only way we can try and make this work."

At that moment, the waitress brought our drinks over. Abbie thanked her, and I took a sip of my diet coke. I knew she was right. It didn't mean I liked the way the conversation was headed, but I got it.

"I get it. You're right, I haven't been the best husband, or father for that matter. I want to make this right too."

Abbie rubbed both palms down her jeans. "Me too. For now, let's agree that we live apart, but we could be good to each other. Talk. Really talk."

I wanted to tell her to come back home, that I missed her, needed her. Instead, I'd need to meet her halfway. "You're right."

"I am?"

"Yeah." Now it was my time to stare out the window.

Abbie sighed. "Thanks," attempted a smile. "That wasn't how I thought this would go today."

We laughed. "So, how's it all going in your new place?"

"That's another story for another time."

Sounded like it wasn't always a happy family living with her sister. I didn't tell her that gave me hope, hope that she'd come home, soon.

Our food arrived. "I'll go get the girls." Abbie disappeared to find them.

My pocket buzzed. I pulled out my phone and stared at the screen. Rae Swanson.

I swiped it. "Rae."

"Jack."

"What's the go?"

"We're going through the stuff from when we tossed Slavosky's place. There's a lot of stuff. Turned up a few things."

My chest surged. "Like what?" I got up and out of the seat and headed for the front door.

"Like dozens more pictures. Nasty stuff."

"Where did you find them?"

"In the attic. In locked boxes. Tied up with ribbon. Weirdo."

"What are you telling me?"

"There's a ton more victims none of us knew about."

"Give me a figure, some idea."

"Dozens of girls from the local area. Thirty, maybe more."

I felt sick. The smell of the food turned my stomach. I opened the front door. Needed air.

"I can be there in an hour." I pushed open the front door and took in a mouthful of air.

"That's not why I'm calling, Jack."

I stopped, found a bench outside, an overflowing ashtray beside it. Sat down. My chest began its clickety clack, banging out a rhythm against my rib cage.

"I'm not sure how to say this."

"How about you just say it then?"

A pause. "I saw the pictures in your wallet. Some of these girls look a lot like your daughters. Your youngest especially,"

I dropped the phone on the bench. Heard Swanson's name calling me. Couldn't talk. My stomach curdled and the earth spun. I put my head between my knees, waiting for the world to right itself. Then I sat back up and took a deep breath. I needed to walk.

The front door squeaked. Abbie stuck her head through the door. I rubbed my hands through my hair.

"Are you okay?"

"I'm not sure."

"What happened?"

I couldn't tell her what had happened. Not when we'd come so far. Maybe soon, but at that moment, I decided to shield my wife from the news.

"A hiccup in the case."

"Looks like it's more than that."

I stood up. "I could use a hug if you're up for it."

She eyed me, blinking. Then stepped towards me and held me for a long moment.

I stepped away. "Thanks," I said.

"Come on, the girls are back, the food's getting cold."

"I'll be there in a minute, I promise. I'll just finish off this call."

Abbie shot me a worried look before heading inside to the warm sanctuary of Rosa's. I shoved my hands in my pockets and sat back down on the bench.

I'd thought it was wrapped up, merely a formality. This was the last thing I had ever expected. A threat to my family. Had he hurt the girls? Or were Jones and McElroy stalking them, scoping them out as prospects?

I picked up the phone.

"Hello?"

"Yeah, Jack, I'm still here. I'm sorry, I wanted to tell you in person but...Garrett told me you were seeing your wife and kids today. He told me what happened."

"You did the right thing telling me."

"Look, there's no evidence he did anything other than take pictures of some of these girls, yours included."

"Yeah. Look I gotta go, the food's going cold."

"I understand. Take care. I'll call you later, okay? Maybe tonight."

"Thanks," I hung up and tucked the phone away inside my jacket pocket. I walked towards the front entrance and opened the glass door. I needed to somehow draw a line in the sand between this job, and my life, my wife, my kids.

But then this job was like nothing else in my career. It had taken a chunk out of me. As I walked back inside towards my smiling, beautiful family, I thought about the fact that as homicide detectives, sometimes we got lucky, we won, we'd find the bad guy, lock him away and throw away the key... but in the process, we lost a part of ourselves forever.

Don't miss out!

Visit the website below and you can sign up to receive emails whenever Andrea Drew publishes a new book. There's no charge and no obligation.

https://books2read.com/r/B-A-PFGB-RINY

BOOKS 2 READ

Connecting independent readers to independent writers.

Did you love *A Thousand Cuts*? Then you should read *Sentinel Rising* by Andrea Drew!

Two Families. One Secret. Powers worth hiding.

Lauren Whitehouse, mother and police wife, has disappeared without a trace, and her sister insists that Lauren's husband had a hand in it.

Detective turned private investigator Connor Reardon wants only one thing: a middle class existence where his Sentinel abilities remain secret. An unspeakable act of violence draws Reardon once again into a world of old-fashioned detective work and supernatural danger, a world he thought he had left behind forever.

Reardon is persuaded to use his unique skills to find the missing woman. As he investigates, he discovers there are terrible secrets connected to her, and dangerous men behind her.

To solve the mystery, he and his fiance, Gypsy Shields, must undertake a journey that requires him to navigate a web of lies, betrayal, and treachery, and come face to face with the darkness within himself.

If you like a good whodunnit with a paranormal slant like the shows "Medium" and "Ghost Whisperer," you'll love Sentinel Rising.

Read more at www.andreadrewauthor.com.

Also by Andrea Drew

DS Jack Fletcher
A Thousand Cuts

The Gypsy Medium Series
Gypsy Hunted
Gypsy Cradle
Gypsy Curse
Gypsy Life
Sentinel Rising
The Gypsy Medium series boxed set (1-4)
Shikhari Connection

Watch for more at www.andreadrewauthor.com.

About the Author

Andrea Drew has been a commercial copy writer and resume writer for over a decade.

She's written for celebrity stylists, assisted business coaches and start-ups, written grants for not for profits, delivered marketing presentations to business owners, and attends Australian writing conventions. Her self-published book "Pro Resumes Made Easy" has been downloaded over 40,000 times.

Andrea has one husband (more than enough), three kids, a pet rock (her daughters not hers), and a house in the suburbs, where she's hard at work on the second novel in the Gypsy series. Email her at andrea@andrea-drew.com.

Read more at www.andreadrewauthor.com.